THE PIRATE PRINCESS
RETURN TO THE EMERALD ISLE

Matthew McCafferty Morris

red beard publishing

Published by Red Beard Publishing, LLC, Norwalk CT, in 2013.
mmm@redbeardpublishing.com
ISBN 978-0989088701

For Katie, Anessa, and Connor

Find your treasure, it's out there.

Preface

This work is the product of travels in the country of my ancestors, my absolute fascination with its history and people, and a soul-shattering period of being laid off from work for the second time in my life.

I was completely bored with the internet and decided one day to challenge myself to write a book. I have loved writing ever since some really dedicated teachers forced me to do it as a child and told me I was good at it. I had been writing a blog for a few years and thought it was time to step it up a notch. My idea was to write a story that introduced some Irish mythology and history into an adventure tale about a girl modeled after my daughters, because they needed a role model that wasn't a princess. Well, not exactly.

I needed a beginning.

Some very dear friends of mine, the O'Farrells, had told me a story of "the knock" as it occurred to them in real life. I had loved the story from the moment I heard it, and it was the perfect way for me to start this semi-magical story. It began with a *Boom* and from that point forward I was amazed at how, at any time I needed a setting or story element, it magically appeared in a Google or Wikipedia search for me. It was as though I was being fed this story from the otherworld. In just four weeks I had written the entire book and then spent the next couple of years polishing and working on it. The hardest thing was that, as I neared completion, I finally found a job and it took away almost all of my time for writing. Here it is nonetheless.

I want to thank my wife Christie for standing by me and supporting our entire family during the layoffs and for putting up with a crazy husband who thought he could be an author. I want to thank Ireland and its people for being such a magical place and inspiration to me since my first trip there with my grandmother on her first time back "home" just before she passed away and my numerous trips there afterward. I want to thank my parents Bonnie and Bill, who said it was just as good as any book they had ever read. My cousin Mike Reid, my first editor, whose excitement about my book really boosted my confidence and whose thoughtful insight brought it to another level completely. My early readers, Tony, Vikki, Fidelma, Rick, Diane, and a few others I may have left out who bolstered my confidence as well because no one ever said it stunk. And finally, I want to thank my editor Stephanie J. Beavers, whose careful review polished my work to where it is now.

Thank you for reading,

Matthew Morris

THE PIRATE PRINCESS
RETURN TO THE EMERALD ISLE

1

Midnight Adventure

Where am I?

Green…

Everywhere she looked, green was in a thousand shades, undulating, pulsing, living green, but nothing was particularly clear. It was like staring at a kaleidoscope made especially for St. Patrick's Day: green and green and green. She tried to focus on something, anything, but her eyes weren't working right.

Concentrate, Meg.

She couldn't really see, but thought she could feel. She dialed her mind to her sense of touch. She could feel something all around her body. It was a cold feeling, not dry and not wet, either. Mist? Was it a cool mist that chilled her skin? She tried harder to focus.

Where was she?

Slowly, as though someone in the green mist turned up the volume, a sound became clear all around her. It was faint at first but grew louder the more she relied on her sense of hearing. With her mind, she grasped at the sound like she would a rope thrown from the side of a boat, and pulled her thoughts towards it. It was a sound as familiar to her as her mother's voice: waves crashing on the shore.

When she scrunched her toes in delight with the excitement of recognizing what she was hearing she felt smooth grains of sand. She looked down and could make out her bare feet on a beach. Finally she was seeing something real. The wind was blowing her hair, and when she looked up she saw she was on a strange and rocky shoreline, in a place she did not know.

Ahead of her on the beach, hunched over and walking with a stick, she saw an old man in a tattered grey suit looking out upon the sea as he moved along. She could see the man and what he was doing, but when she tried to focus on him it was as if the lights had gone out and she was thrown back in the dizzying green mist.

It took a while at first, but she figured out that she had to bring her senses back one at a time, as she did before, sight, hearing, and touch. Then she would be back on the beach with the old man. She tried to see who it was again only to be thrown back into the green nothingness. After doing this a couple of times she stopped trying to focus on the man and just walked towards the figure, keeping him in the corner of her vision. She quickened her pace but no matter how fast she walked he remained just ahead of her.

"Sir," she called out. "Excuse me, sir?" As soon as they left her lips the words she spoke faded in the roar of the ocean waves.

Although she could not see exactly what the old man was doing, he seemed to be looking for something and she felt for him strongly. Her heart was heavy for his longing and she didn't know why. He was definitely looking out to sea for something.

She looked out on the ocean to where the man was gazing and, strangely enough, she was able to focus on the long, curved line that was the horizon on the water. Timidly at first, for fear of being thrown back into the green mist, she stared at the moving sea, increasing her attention bit by bit.

It was grey and white, rising and lowering with great waves and, faintly, just at that point where the grey ocean met the blue sky, she saw a wisp of black emerge out of nowhere. As happened when looking at the man, if she concentrated on the black form she saw nothing. Out of the corners of her eyes, however, she was easily able to make out what appeared to be some dark clouds looming in the distance.

A storm? She turned to the man on the shore to confirm her suspicion, but when she looked back he was gone and so was everything.

She was back in the green mist and could not feel or hear a thing.

Boom!

The noise filled Meg's room. It was a bang or knock or something and whatever it was, it was really loud. She sat straight up in bed with an indrawn breath. Her heart was pounding and her spine tingling. *What in the world was that?*

Meg's head was still heavy from the strange dream but she was now wide awake and very frightened. She looked around her room to see what could have possibly made the loud noise that scared her awake. Nothing had fallen off her dresser or the shelves. The room was lit by a silvery glow that came from her window, just around the corner from her bed. She looked around again. Nothing was out of place, but…Finn!

Her comforter showed an indentation where her dog would normally be lying, but Finn was nowhere to be found.

Where did that dog go? The bedroom door was closed, as was the closet, so he had to be in her room somewhere. Meg got out of bed and walked towards the moonlight streaming from the alcove and sure enough, she found her big white dog. He was on his hind legs leaning on the windowsill with his ears perked up searching for whatever it was that made the terrible crash that woke them both.

Meg stood next to Finn at the window and looked out on the full moon shining its light on the water beyond her back yard, as a gentle breeze was leading the trees in a slow dance back and forth. The peaceful scene calmed her nerves a little, but going back to bed was not an option at this point because she was wide awake and very curious. She had to find what woke her.

"Come on, boy," Meg said to her dog, and headed towards the bedroom door. A tree or something must have fallen on the house; she was sure of it. She reached out and twisted the warm brass knob. She opened the door and poked her head out.

Nothing… No lights were on and no one was out in the hallway.

Someone else had to have heard it.

She grabbed Finn's collar and lead him to her little brother's bedroom, right next to hers. The old hinges let out a creak as she pushed the door open, but even that noise didn't wake up the little boy who was sleeping peacefully in his crib.

Are you kidding me? It didn't even wake the baby!

She went farther down the hall, making two more stops along the way. It was the same situation with her parents and her big sister: All were sleeping undisturbed in their beds, oblivious to the natural disaster that must have struck their old house.

Was it the dream? No way! It could not have been the dream because Finn heard it too. A branch or a limb from one of the tall trees in the yard had to have fallen on the roof, and her family was going to be very surprised to find out they had slept through such a racket. This could not wait until morning. She had to find out what had made that crash, and so she headed downstairs.

Meg quietly made her way to the first floor, the loud knock still echoing in her head. The house was completely silent and eerily bright from the moonlight. She looked out the window next to the front door and saw nothing out of the ordinary.

"Let's go out back," she whispered to Finn.

As she tiptoed down the hall towards the kitchen, the tick tacking of Finn's paws on the hardwood floors sounded like fire crackers in the silent house. She shushed him and he gave her a confused look in return. They walked through the kitchen and found nothing. Meg decided that they had better go outside to look at the house from afar so as to survey the damage that must have happened. Meg slid the heavy glass patio door open with a rumble and walked out into the autumn night, her dog close behind.

The wind blew her hair as she stepped onto the stone patio and had a flashback to the strange dream that had tingled her senses. Unlike her dream, though, the peaceful sounds of chirping crickets and waves gently lapping the shore greeted her. It was soft and comforting, broken only by the ringing of a navigational bell rolling over the water from a buoy in the distance.

This was exciting. Meg had never been outside of her house alone at night and she was extremely alert. As in her dream, she became acutely aware of all her senses. The breeze that moved the trees and tousled her hair carried with it the smells of salt water and the decaying leaves that were everywhere in her yard. It was a strange, earthy-ocean combination. She walked across the patio towards the backyard which gently slanted down to the water's edge.

The moon was spectacular. It lit everything outside in a bright, silvery-blue glow from its spot in the sky just above Fishers Island. A streak of reflected moonlight ran across the water from the shore to the island in the distance where Meg's grandmother lived. It looked like a magical bridge suspended on the waves that linked their two islands. Meg shook her head to get back to reality; she was out here for a reason and that reason was to find what caused the crash.

She turned around and was disappointed to see the roof of her home was completely undamaged. No branches or limbs were lying across the Victorian-styled house anywhere.

But the crash had happened! Didn't it?

As if in answer to her question, a stiff gust of wind blew in from the water, startling Meg. She got goose bumps on her skin and felt a sort of tension in the air which made her uncomfortable. Even Finn was uneasy. He was standing tightly against her leg with his ears still perked. He let out a soft whimper. *There had to be something on the other side of the house.* Although she was starting to get a bit scared again, curiosity got the best of her and she pressed on.

Meg and Finn walked around the house, through the grass and leaves, looking up for anything strange or broken at the gabled roofline that rose up and down with its numerous triangular edges that faced out to the sea. There was magic to the fall night around them. The temperature was cool, but not enough to chill Meg, and all of the sounds and smells added to the mystery that surrounded her walk. She expected to find the source of the crash at every turn of the corner, but by the time they had walked all around the house and found nothing, they were back at their starting point on the patio, and Meg decided to give up the search. *Maybe it was her imagination? Maybe it was the dream?*

She walked back inside, puzzled by the night. Her father was standing at the door to the kitchen as she slid the patio door closed.

"What are you doing, honey?" He looked at her over crossed arms. "It's the middle of the night and you should not be outside by yourself."

"Daaad," Meg replied in the sing-songy way only a little girl can address her father, "I was checking out a loud crash that woke us up, aaand I *am* almost eleven and can go outside by myself!"

"Even tomorrow when you turn eleven you are not allowed to go outside by yourself at night. And the only sound that woke me up was the sound of the sliding door to the patio opening." He looked at Meg under totally forced, furrowed brows and a little smirk that showed he was not really mad at her.

"You didn't hear that earth-shattering knock, like something hit our house?"

"No, sweetie," said her father. He reached into the refrigerator and poured a glass of milk which he handed to her, "It must have been a dream, and it's time to go back to bed. We have a big day ahead of us tomorrow."

"But, Dad… even Finn heard it," she said, gulping down the milk and placing the cup in the sink. Her father looked down at the dog and Finn wagged his tail back. He scratched Finn's head in return.

"Maybe you knocked one of the dolls off your bed and onto the floor?"

"I don't sleep with dolls anymore, Daddy!"

He swept her up in his arms and started back upstairs. "I can't believe my little baby doesn't sleep with her dolls anymore. It seems like just yesterday there was a virtual stuffed-animal army at the foot of your bed standing guard over you, but now my big eleven-year-old is all grown up and doesn't need them anymore."

"I have Finn now, Daddy... and will always have you guarding me!"

That put a big smile on her dad's face. He walked Meg into her room then lowered her into bed. She pulled up the sheets and her dad gave her a kiss. "Sweet dreams," he said as he walked out, shutting the door behind him.

"It had to be something, huh, Finn?" she said to her dog as he snuggled in at the foot of her bed. Finn looked up at her with his big dark eyes in agreement. After some tossing and turning the two eventually fell back to sleep.

2

The Big Day

Margaret Grace Murphy woke up after a restless night. Even though it was her eleventh birthday she didn't feel very festive and she had slept in a lot longer than she normally would have on her big day. She stood at the window while getting dressed to see if there was something in the daylight that would explain the crash she had heard in the night. From what she could see there was not a trace of anything that could have produced the incredibly loud knock on the old sea captain's house she lived in. The sunlight felt warm through the glass. As Meg bent down to tie her shoes, the sun brought out the deep red tint in her auburn hair as it dangled in her face.

Finn came over and looked out the window beside her. "I know, Finn..." Meg pointed to the ceiling, "Let's go up to the captain's walk to look around." They walked down the hall to the door through which a steep, crooked stairway led to the attic. She rarely went up there nowadays because it was dusty and creepy, but that crash had rung in her head all night and she knew she would be able to see everything from the little window box on the top of their house.

A regular feature on old houses in seaside towns was a cupola and platform on the roof. Meg knew her cupola was called a *captain's walk* and she had to constantly correct the neighborhood kids who called it a *widow's watch*. Some of the meaner kids who picked on her because she was short, liked to tell her that her house was haunted and that they could see the ghost of a widow on moonlit nights. Had the illiterate kids that roamed her street ever taken time out to read the historical plaque on the house, they would have known that the sea captain who built it lived there his entire life with his family and that his wife had died before him. But, in Meg's head, the damage was done—just the thought of a ghostly widow kept her out of the attic regardless how uninformed the story was.

The attic was full of plastic storage bins and miscellaneous pieces of furniture. Cobwebs hung from the rafters of the roof. They walked towards the center of the house where four wood beams surrounded an old wood ladder that was fixed from the floor to the roof box. Meg had to leave Finn behind as she climbed the ladder. Its rungs had been worn down as smooth as stone from a hundred years of use and barely creaked as she ascended.

Inside the cupola there was a bench built into the wall for sitting on rainy days and a hatch that led outside to a small wrap-around porch. Meg crawled through the hatch and, as she stood up, she gazed out on a beautiful fall day. There was not a cloud in the sky and she could see for miles in every direction. The view, however, did not distract her from doing what she had come up to do; Meg carefully scanned the immediate area and could not find a single downed tree. The large oak and pine trees stood proudly beside the house as they had done seemingly forever. There not a single thing on top of the house that could have made that noise.

Meg thought she must have dreamed the whole crash the night before. She soaked up the beautiful scenery around her and breathed in the salty air.

The sunlight danced on the water of Long Island Sound—*the Sound*, as they called it—and there were no boats to be seen. In the distance, like a gray wall, the whole of Long Island, New York protected the small body of water they lived on from the great Atlantic Ocean. Meg's house was on an island in the Mystic River. She gazed on the water and, for just a moment, thought she saw some storm clouds just past Long Island, but they instantly disappeared into the blue sky, leaving nothing but a strange feeling in Meg's stomach. A train horn blew from up the river breaking Meg's trance. She looked back towards the town of Mystic and its drawbridge. The view of the town from her captain's walk was almost as beautiful as the view of the water. Before the thoughts of ghosts had frightened her, she used to come up on sunny days to read and to look at the quintessential New England seaside village where she lived. The old buildings and houses that lined both sides of the Mystic River fueled her appetite for reading and history as much as did the tall ships in the famous seaport museum. She decided that next summer she would start coming back up here again with her e-reader and stop letting the imaginary ghosts of others keep her from such an amazing place where she could read and dream.

The drawbridge in town was up. Meg was reminded of spending the day before in the village with her family, something they rarely did. Her parents had had business to attend to in town that morning. Afterwards, they had lunch at the famous Mystic Pizza shop where a Hollywood movie was filmed. They then stopped for ice cream and sat by the bridge to watch the tourists. It was a nice morning and the tourists were as crazy as usual, but it ended way too fast. They had to hurry back to Masons Island so Meg's dad could go out and turn some trawls before nighttime.

Meg's father was a lobsterman. He captained a small boat in the waters of the sound. Where they lived, being a lobsterman was once a very profitable occupation, but there was a big die-off of lobsters in the late 90s that hurt the business. The die-off was blamed on a number of things, including pollution, low oxygen levels, and even a parasite, but no one was absolutely sure. Lobstermen went from 'eating steaks to eating rice overnight,' as they used to say, and many ended up getting out of the business. Not Meg's dad. Mark Murphy kept at it and, just when the lobsters started to make a comeback and business started to get a little better for him, they died off again. This second time around there was a fear that spraying for mosquitoes to prevent West Nile Virus is what had killed them. Although he was not making the big bucks he had made in the past, Meg's father kept on lobstering because it was all he had ever wanted to do.

"Meg!" She heard her mother's voice calling out from downstairs.

Her family! She totally forgot about them.

Meg crawled back through the hatch, down the ladder, and scurried downstairs with her dog in tow. Shay Murphy was at the bottom of the stairs waiting for her. "Here she is!" she called out, "our big eleven year old!" Although she was short, Shay was incredibly strong—she swam in fast currents—and easily lifted Meg up in the air, carrying her to the kitchen where her sister and brother were already having breakfast.

Meg's mother was beautiful, with jet black hair and slate blue eyes that were very calculating. She was also fisherman, but one of a different sort: Shay was a scallop diver. Using scuba gear, she dove down into the cold ocean and the nasty currents of "The Race," an area of water which separates Long Island, New York from coastal Connecticut. There she handpicked the popular bivalve from the ocean floor. This method of fishing produced a scallop that was less gritty than those that were dredged from a boat. Her cleaner diver's scallops allowed her to price them much higher than the commercial ones. Diving for them was also a very environmentally good way to fish because handpicking the scallops did not disturb the seabed as much as a giant dredge would, which was another strong selling point for Shay's scallops.

Meg's big sister Eileen was eating waffles and watching their little brother Sean crumble a blueberry muffin on the tray in front of him and then throw it on the floor.

"Happy birthday, Meg!" she said. Eileen was fourteen years old, tall and lean, with her blond hair up in its usual ponytail.

Sean was almost two. He said something that sounded like "day-day," and gave Meg a big smile while holding his hands up in the air to be rescued from his high chair.

"Thank you," Meg said to Eileen. She then patted her brother on his sandy-blond head and added, "Sorry, Sean. No escape yet."

Meg's dad was sitting at the counter reading a newspaper and sipping on coffee. He looked up at her and said, "Come here and give me a big hug, my little midnight explorer." She walked up to him and he squeezed her tightly, "I remember when you were born. You were so small I could hold you in my hands." He held up his big, strong hands as if he was cradling an egg.

"I was not that small, Daddy!"

"You were! You were born five weeks early and the tiniest little thing. You just couldn't wait to join our family, and rushed yourself out before you were done cooking." He squeezed her again, "You were put in the newborn intensive care unit right after you were born, so your little lungs could finish developing. I know you don't remember, but your sister spent every day staring into your incubator praying that we take her little sister home. And finally, two long weeks later, we did! " Meg's premature birth had left her always a little smaller than the other kids her age, and although perfectly healthy, she sometimes found herself a bit short of breath when doing strenuous activities.

Meg rolled her eyes and scoffed at the story she had heard a million times before saying, "Yeah, yeah...But seriously, I can't believe none of you heard that crash last night. It shook my bed and I swear I thought the roof was caved in by a tree."

The blank stares of her family were the only response she got back. Finally her mother said, "I'm sure you heard something, honey, but the rest of us are such heavy sleepers, we could probably sleep through a hurricane. Did you find anything outside on your little midnight adventure?"

"Nothing. But I know I heard something," frustrated, she looked at her family a moment more and then sat down for breakfast. Her mom had made her favorite, a bacon sandwich on white bread with home-fried potatoes on the side, which she ate happily while talking about the big crash with her sister and brother.

If it were any other day, Meg's father would have been long gone lobstering. He usually got on the boat a couple of hours before dawn to haul down to his boat the mackerel, bunker, or any other cheap fish that was being thrown away by other fisherman. He then stuffed bait bags with the rotting fish which were used to lure crustaceans into big wire traps. After filling the bait bags, he took a lonely cruise out to the sound where his trawls lay.

Trawls were a string of lobster traps all tied together, with a buoy at each end. He would haul the trawls out of the water one at a time, unload the legal-sized lobsters into his tank, and throw any undersized or egg-carrying females back overboard, along with any other creature that was drawn to the decaying fish in the trap. It was a hard job for one man to do by himself. In the good old days he used to have a deck hand to help. But the number of good lobsters that he pulled out every day was not enough to sustain both him and a deck hand.

Meg looked up at her father and smiled. She was happy to have him home for a whole day, as he rarely took that much time off. "The traps can't bait themselves," he always reminds them. Although Mark Murphy always managed to tweak his schedule to be at anything his kids were doing, birthdays were the rare treat. Five times a year they were lucky to have him to themselves all day long.

"So what's the schedule today, Daaad—?" She almost said *Daddy*, but was trying to be more adult lately.

"Finish your breakfast, and then we will do some chores before we load up your mom's boat."

"Chores!" said Meg, "But it's my birthday!" She looked up at her dad with her best puppy dog eyes, but he didn't flinch. "What do we have to do today?" she said. Chores around their house varied from simple house cleaning to mending lobster traps.

"I still haven't changed all of the vents to the new size the DEP wants," Mark said, referring to the plastic escape vents attached to the traps.

Lobster traps are metal cages with a string net on the inside in the shape of a funnel, called a *head*. On the big side of the head there are two open sides in the cage that allow the lobsters to crawl in and up through a small hole leading them into the *salon* in the back of the cage, where bait is held and where the lobsters are trapped. The escape vents are detachable, rectangular plastic holes on two sides of the salon that allow smaller animals to escape. The size of the vents were mandated by the Department of Environmental Protection—the DEP—and changed as the DEP changed the size of lobsters that could legally be caught. In trying to grow back the population of lobsters, the DEP had been making the vents bigger and bigger to allow ever older, larger lobsters to escape back to the waters to survive and multiply for longer periods of time.

"How many trawls?" Eileen whined.

"Just two. We should be done in a jiffy," said Mark with a smile.

Each trawl had ten traps, which meant they would have to switch out forty vents before they would be able to leave. With three of them working on it, however, it would not take long. Shay stayed behind in the house with Sean, while Meg, Eileen, and Mark went down to the dock to work.

There was nothing quite like being out on the dock in the morning. The water was like glass and the air was still crisp from the night before. Nothing was on the sound but the seabirds. The sound of their footsteps on the wood pier caused an egret to take flight, its graceful image reflecting back on the still water as it flew out of sight. A flock of seagulls floating on the water cawed in the distance.

Meg's parents had bought their house mostly because it had its own dock, but they also loved the history it held as an old whaling captain's house. They named the house "Sweet Haven," because people who lived near the water liked to name their houses. As a kid, Meg's father loved Popeye the Sailor. He knew that Sweet Haven was the town where the cartoon character had lived, and he even had the habit of calling his own kids "Sweet Pea," like the baby in Popeye. Shay even looked a little like Olive Oyl with her jet black hair. A hand-carved wood sign that said "Sweet Haven" was nailed to one of the pilings, and the dock that floated on the water was covered with trawls.

The trawls were laid out on benches and Mark, Eileen, and Meg quickly set to work with clippers and plastic straps, snipping the old vents off and strapping the new vents on. Mark started on one end and Meg and Eileen were at the other. It always ended up in a race to see who could do more as they worked toward the trawls in the center.

While they were working, Eileen looked at Meg over a trap and said, "I can't believe you went outside alone last night. What were you thinking?" Meg's big sister had a menacing look on her face.

"Didn't you listen to me at breakfast? I just wanted to find out what had made the big crashing noise that woke me up."

Eileen looked down. "How did Dad find out you were outside?" she whispered.

"He heard me open the patio door. Why do you care?"

"Forget about it," said Eileen. Meg could tell that she was making a mental note about something.

As always, their father did twice as many vents by himself as the two sisters did together, winning the race. Just as they finished the last trap, Shay came down to the dock with Sean and a bag filled with everything they would need for a day on the water. Meg's mother was always prepared for anything, and the "day bag" for sailing was a huge, waterproof duffel bag filled with food, foul-weather gear, and other things Shay thought they might need. She brought the day bag aboard every time they went on the boat, no matter how long they were going to be out. Sometimes Meg thought her mother was silly carrying all that stuff, because they rarely used any of it. But Shay always said that she would rather be safe than sorry, and made sure the day bag was jammed with safety equipment.

They loaded up the sailboat and soon cast off of their dock for the short trip to Nanny's on Fishers Island, across the sound from their house.

3

Sailing

It was really quite warm for the middle of October. The family only needed light clothes and windbreakers for the short sail across Fishers Island Sound, the smaller body of water that separated their island from the one that their grandmother lived on. The wind was up and the boat was moving fast.

Kathleen "Nanny" Sullivan had emigrated from Ireland to Connecticut and had "found" Fishers Island on a sailing excursion with her husband Sean long ago. The island's stone walls, few trees, and windswept moors looked exactly like her home in Ireland; it had got that look after a hurricane devastated the island in the 1800s. From the first time she set foot on shore, Nanny felt right at home and decided then and there that Fishers Island was the place she was going to live and raise a family.

Sean Sullivan wasn't so sure. They had only been married a short time and he was still getting used to living in America that day they had sailed out to the island. Being isolated on an island was not his first choice as a place to settle, and he had just started a job with his cousin to learn the building trade, but Kathleen always got her way. Shay always said her mother could convince a bird to walk across town instead of fly. He agreed to give it a try. Sean was able to find work for the many "old money" families who summered on the island. He was a farmer's son who had also learned enough carpentry to make a decent living by both gardening and taking care of the estates that dotted the island. Kathleen easily found work at the yacht club on Fishers, teaching the sailing skills that she had learned as a little girl while growing up on the hard, west coast of Ireland. She taught Shay, their only child, everything she knew.

The sound that separates Fishers Island from Connecticut is a hazard-filled body of water. There are numerous reefs, shoals, and boulder patches that rise abruptly from the sea floor, any of which could easily strand or sink a boat. But Shay Murphy had been diving and sailing these waters since she was a child, and she knew every inch of the seabed like she knew her children. A less-skilled sailor would never be able to follow the path Shay charted from Mystic to Wilderness Point on the island, but she loved to challenge herself and her boat, the *Muirín* (pronounced *mur-een*).

The *Muirín* (which means *scallop* in Gaelic, the Irish language) was a New Haven Sharpie sailboat with a cat-ketch rig. Before the age of power, this type of sailboat was very popular for oystering on the east coast of America, but is considered old-fashioned nowadays. A typical sailboat is a single-masted *sloop* with two triangular sails. The smaller sail in the front is called the *headsail* or *jib* and the larger one in the rear is called the *mainsail*. On a sloop, the mast is in the center of the boat. The *cat-ketch* has a single mast towards the *bow* (the front of the boat) with one sail, and a slightly smaller *mizzen* mast towards the *aft* (the rear of the boat). The cat-ketch rig used to be very popular on work boats in the old days but fell out of style as sailboats became leisure craft.

Different sailboats all have advantages and disadvantages, and sailors are particular regarding the type of boat they prefer. Shay Murphy loved the *Muirín* with her two masts and gentle sailing ways. There was a reason the New Haven Sharpie was the choice for work boats: It could be rigged by one person in under five minutes and sailed alone just as easily. The *Muirín* also had a shallow draft which helped Shay to use it as her fishing boat. She would sail it out to a reef or shoal, drop the sails, and anchor the boat while she dove beneath the waters to handpick the scallops.

Meg's mother had started scuba diving at a young age. Nanny said that Shay had seen Jacques Cousteau, the underwater explorer, on TV one Saturday morning and begged and begged them until they gave her scuba lessons. After one dive in Fishers Island Sound she was hooked, and Shay spent any free time she had under the water with a tank on her back. Scuba had been just a hobby until she read about scallop diving and decided to see if she could turn her passion into a job. She was one of the first scallop divers in Connecticut. It was a rough go at first, but Shay's diver's scallops developed a devoted following at local restaurants, and eventually scallop diving became a successful business for her. Using a sailboat as a fishing vessel removed the price of fuel from the bottom line and made her diver's scallops even more profitable.

Shay had been at the tiller of a sailboat her whole life. With a sailing instructor for a mother and a home on an island, she didn't have much choice. Nanny started teaching her sailing at a young age, and they spent a lot of their free time under billowing *sheets*, or sails, cruising along the shores of Connecticut and New York. They sailed so often and loved it so much that they made a vow to each other that they would only travel on the water in a vessel with sails. Since Shay had spent so much of her life on, or diving below, the water, it was only natural for her to raise her children from the helm of a sailboat just as she had been.

Meg absolutely loved being on the *Muirín*. Unlike her father's boat, that smelled of diesel and was as loud as anything, the *Muirín* was whisper quiet and had just the smell of hardwood and the sound of the sea. Since sailing was in her blood, at the age of four and following in the footsteps of her mother and grandmother, Meg had also made the vow to never travel on the water in a motor boat. Mark was astounded at his little girl's declaration. But from that point on, she never set foot in her father's boat or, for that matter, any boat with an engine, much to his consternation.

The *Muirín* was Meg's sanctuary. She had been sailing in her since she was a baby, strapped to a special seat at the helm, a seat that was now occupied by her baby brother Sean. The rolling and rocking of the boat was the most comforting feeling she knew and the salt air held the smell of home to her. Meg's love of the water was as much a part of her as her love for her family, and she wanted to spend every minute she could on or near the water.

Meg's whole family loved the water except Eileen, who was the only land lover of the family. She preferred to be on her bike, on a stage dancing, or doing just about any activity that she could on land. It wasn't that Eileen hated the sea; she had grown up on it like they all had, but she just had too many things to do on land to waste time floating around on the water. Even so, Eileen had enough salt water in her blood that even she felt at ease while sailing on the *Muirín*.

Because it was her birthday, Meg was at the tiller and in control of the boat. In fact, as soon as Meg knew the difference between a *close haul* and a *beam reach*, Shay had allowed her to man the helm whether it was her birthday or not. All her mom would do during these trips would be to tell Meg how and where to navigate, but Meg knew what she was doing. With her own lifelong sailing experience and great instructors, Meg eventually knew as much as her mom and Nanny did about this body of water and didn't need much help. She quickly learned to navigate around the sound in almost any wind and tidal condition.

They sailed across Fishers Island Sound and then followed the northern shore of the island past Chocomount Cove and West Harbor. The wind was stiff and the sailing was fast, but Meg handled the boat like an artist with a brush.

Meg felt completely alive at these moments. Hair blowing in the wind and the salty water misting in her face, it was as close to heaven as a girl could get, at least a girl with seafaring blood like Meg. She kept a close eye on the *telltales,* or *tattle tales* as she liked to call them, which were small pieces of fabric attached to the *luff,* or leading edge of the sail. Sailors used the telltales as indicators of how efficiently the wind moved over the sheet. If the green telltale towards the top was streaming and the red one at the bottom was fluttering, Meg knew she needed to tighten up the sheet to get better speed. She kept one hand on the tiller, the other on the lines that controlled the sheets, and her eyes on the course she needed to take.

Each part of the course is called a *leg*, and each leg has a landmark towards which the boat is steered. As they sailed across the sound, the wind was on the *port*, or left, side of the boat. When the wind is on that side it is called a *beam reach*. No matter which way a sailor is turned, port is always the left-hand side of the boat, looking forward to the bow and starboard is always the right. Meg's first landmark was Chocomount Cove, which she kept in sight over the bow. She just had to tweak her course every now and again to avoid certain things she had been trained to look for on the surface of the water.

Shay had taught Meg to read the water like a book. Meg was always looking ahead for *cat's paw patches*, where a light wind ripples the surface of the water and could cause her to lose speed. When the waves in front of the sailboat went from long and slow to short and fast, Meg knew that the seabed was closer to the surface of the water and that she had to avoid the shallow water. This is called wave *shoaling*. Meg knew to read these and other signs from the surface of the water to help her on the course she was sailing.

As she turned starboard off of the island's shore, the wind was now directly behind the boat. This left Meg a couple of options on how to approach the next leg. She could turn the boat so that the wind was directly aft of the boat, and let out each sail as far as they could go on both sides so that they looked like a pair of wings. This is called *butterflying*. It was not her best option because a shift in the wind could cause one of the sails and its boom to violently swing in the opposite direction in an accidental *jibe,* which could snap the rigging, or worse, knock someone overboard. Shay and Meg only butterflied when they were alone and only with perfect wind. Meg decided instead to keep the wind on a *broad reach,* or just slanting to the rear of the *Muirín,* and start jibing towards the North and South Dumpling islands, her next landmark. It was a little slower but much safer.

North Dumpling Island was a local legend. It was owned by the famous inventor of the Segway, the two-wheeled, self-balancing personal transporter. He had turned an old lighthouse into his residence and the island into a small compound. When the government turned down an attempt by him to build a wind turbine to power the island, he jokingly seceded from United States and refers to his property as the Kingdom of North Dumpling. The eccentric inventor even had a replica of Stonehenge built on the northeastern corner of the island. Meg kept this in her sight while doing controlled jibes port and starboard of the wind.

The chain of islands the Murphy family lived around started in the sound and ended up in the ocean at the very popular Block Island. Fishers Island, where Nanny lived, was secluded and did not get the large number of visitors that Block Island, the next island up the east coast, received. Both islands were first charted in 1614 by Dutch explorer Adrian Block who named the larger island after himself. The smaller island, Nanny's, was named either for Block's First Mate Mr. Visscher or for the local Pequots who fished on this island they called *Munnawtawkin,* meaning *place of observation.* The Native American name was quite appropriate for Fishers

Island, and the Murphy family spent a day every now and then walking around the island "observing" when they visited Nanny. Shay loved to show her kids where she grew up and Mark loved to gawk at the classic cars that traveled the island's roads. There were not many cars on the island, but the few there were all seemed to be the most beautiful old cars from a bygone era.

Meg turned the boat port after passing the Dumplings and headed up the west coast. The wind was now in front of them which made the sailing a little more challenging. Every sailboat has a *no-go zone* when headed *windward*. This is a thirty-to-fifty-degree arc where the wind cannot fill the sails to produce forward motion. When Meg turned the boat into the wind they were in the no-go zone for just a moment, but the boat drifted into a payoff and the wind filled the sheets again.

A close haul is when the boat heads into the wind just slightly to one side of the no-go zone. This is when the telltales come in really handy. When *beating* into the wind, Meg paid close attention to the telltales and pulled the sheets in tightly to get the most efficient air movement, steering as closely to the no-go zone as possible without them *luffing*.

Race Rock Lighthouse was Meg's next landmark. It was in the no-go zone, so she had to turn the boat back and forth into the wind in a zigzag motion called *tacking*. Meg kept the grey stones of the lighthouse in sight as she tacked back and forth towards the most challenging part of their trip: the dangerous channel between Race Point and the Lighthouse.

Race Rock Light, as it is called, is a nineteenth-century stone building that was constructed on a massive concrete and granite turret-like foundation built on top of a reef. With the help of divers who placed riprap on the underwater ledge to level it off above the water, the foundation itself took seven years to complete. The solid foundation was capped with a beautiful, story-and-a-half, solid stone house where the lighthouse keeper was quartered. The keeper's house was connected to a tower that held the light. The lighthouse, in comparison to the foundation, took only nine months to complete, a fact which always amazed Meg. No matter how long it took to build, Race Rock Light was needed to guard boats from The Race, that fast and powerful current that moves in two directions, depending on the tide at the opening of Long Island Sound. The lighthouse was placed off Race Point because of the dangerous reef and rocks below the surface in the area of The Race that had sent many boats to a watery grave before the construction of the lighthouse.

The wind was blowing heavily and the *Muirín* was on a close haul headed to port. Meg could just make out Race Rock Light over the starboard bow when she heard something she had never before heard in her life.

4

An Old Woman on the Rocks

At first Meg thought the sound she heard was the wind, which can sometimes make a noise when whipping through the rigging of a boat. The sound she heard, however, was not coming from the lines on the *Muirín*. From somewhere in the distance she heard a high-pitched wail. It started at a very high pitch that slowly went down and back up in a mournful-sounding cry.

"Do you hear that?" Meg shouted to her family.

"It's just the rigging singing, Sweet Pea," said her father.

"Meg, you know that sound!" added her mother.

"No. It's too loud and it's not coming from our boat," Meg said.

"It is probably coming from that big sloop moored near the shore on the port side," Eileen said, pointing to a beautiful boat anchored just off of the island.

"No. It's coming from the starboard side where there are no boats, and it sounds like a woman crying."

"Meg, honey," Shay said with a big smile, "sound travels very strangely on the water. It bounces off waves and buoys and other things and can trick a sailor into thinking it is coming from somewhere that it is not. It's just the lines on that sloop vibrating with the wind."

Meg's father gave her a kind look and added, "Sounds like the rigging singing are what made old sailors come up with all sorts of tales of mermaids, sirens, and sea monsters when it was just their minds playing tricks on them."

"I know what I am hearing, guys, and it is a woman crying!" Meg defiantly shot back.

"Yeah, like the big crash you heard last night that no one else heard," teased Eileen. The family chuckled. Meg shot her sister a threatening look—she was always teasing her—and Eileen returned the glance by sticking her tongue out at Meg. Eileen wasn't a bad big sister like the ones you see in the movies, but she never made things easy for Meg. She often taunted her and made sure Meg knew who the oldest child was. These two girls with such different hobbies rarely had anything to share with each other. Meg had no interest in dancing and sports, and Eileen had no interest in the sea. Perhaps because of their differences, they usually got along okay, even if it was because they were never in each other's way. But Eileen still bugged Meg at times.

The sound Meg had heard was soon lost in the cacophony of the strong headwind whipping the sails and the waves crashing around them. She concentrated on tacking towards the historic landmark, closely watching the water in front of the boat. The tide was going out, and Meg knew that the huge amount of water emptying through The Race was helping the *Muirín* in its battle of forward motion against the heavy wind. With the tide going out, the headwind was actually a good thing to have at this particular leg. If the wind had been with them, both natural forces would combine to push the boat at top speed towards the underwater reef—the reef the lighthouse warded boats away from. *Beating into the wind* allowed Meg a little more time to execute the maneuvers she knew by heart to get the boat through the rarely used channel. Few boats and captains attempted to go between the point and the rock, but the Murphy girls never steered clear of a challenge.

As they neared Race Rock Light, Shay was the first to spot a woman sitting on the high granite wall that formed the foundation for the light house. "Look at that!" she said. "Some lady must have paddled out to the Race Rock Light."

They all looked and saw a woman sitting on the sea wall. She had long, white hair, and was wearing a flowing, grey dress. Everything about her seemed drab and grey. The wind was blowing her hair and dress in all directions, and it looked as though she was combing her white locks. It was such a strange sight that the whole Murphy family was silent for a moment while they stared. The grey woman was bent over as if she was shielding herself from the wind, so they could not see her face.

"There's no boat tied up to the pier," Shay said, pointing. "It must be a kayaker."

"She's dressed kind of weird for a kayaker," Mark said. "You know, ever since that ghost show on cable did an episode at the lighthouse, there have been all sorts of weirdos sneaking their way on the rock to ghost hunt."

Meg knew what her father was talking about. One night a while back, she heard her father yell and it had woken her up. She wanted to know what he was yelling about, so she went downstairs to snoop. She found him on the edge of the couch talking to the TV. "No way!" he had yelled at the screen, which, to Meg's surprise was in black and white. The image on the screen was a rocking chair in a corner of an attic that started rocking all by itself! Mark explained that the show was using night vision and that it was in the keeper's house of Race Rock Light. He allowed Meg to stay up with him to watch the rest of the show because he said what they were watching was in their own back yard and of interest to her, but Meg always thought he had kept her with him because he was a little scared of the footage. At the time, Meg didn't get what the big deal was; the show had probably rigged a fishing line or something to move the chair (it was on the Sci-Fi channel), but she happily stayed up and watched the rest of the show with her dad. That night came back to her as they sailed past the island.

The air around the *Muirín* seemed to be charged with electricity and the hair on Meg's skin stood on end. She needed to concentrate on where she was going and how to get there; she could not just stop and stare at the sight of the strange woman. When she turned the boat port, into the channel, the wind changed and she was forced to alter her plan mid leg. She tweaked the tiller and pulled in the forward sheet tight while tacking with the aft sail. Meg was able to sneak a peek at the grey woman between tacks, and it was as if her vision had blurred. Although Meg saw the lighthouse and the seawall in perfect focus, the details of the woman's lines were soft and had no definition for her. It was very strange.

Meg could tell her mother was also bothered by the sight of the woman. Shay never took her eyes off the woman as they passed, which showed just how much she trusted Meg to navigate this hazardous spot. This caused Meg to try even harder not to look at the grey woman and just pilot the boat.

The Coast Guard had automated the lighthouse in 1978 and made it off limits to boaters. Shay did what any good captain should do: She radioed in their sighting of the woman on the wall.

"Coast Guard Station, this is the *Muirín*. Over."

"Hi, Shay. What's up?" was the informal reply she received from the voice at the other end of the radio.

"We are just rounding Race Point and see a woman trespassing up on Race Rock Light."

"Thanks, Shay. We'll send out someone to investigate… By the way, could you ask Mark if I can swing by tomorrow and pick up a few lobsters for dinner? Over." Mark smiled and nodded.

"He said 'no problem,' but radio orders cost extra. Over," joked Shay, and they all had a laugh at their family's close connection to the local Coast Guard guys.

Meg heard the wail again over the sound of the wind and she looked back to Race Rock as it grew smaller in the distance. The sight of the grey woman gave her goose bumps. *Was she the one crying?* Meg had steered the boat expertly through the channel in the heavy wind. They were beating against the wind, and Meg was forced to do some tight tacking, swiftly turning the tiller left and then right while trying not to lose momentum or control of the boat. Meg kept the dock of her grandmother's house as her landmark and soon the *Muirín* was tied up at Nanny Sullivan's on Wilderness Point.

5

The Isle of Youth

Nanny Sullivan's house was tucked in the back corner of the property of an estate house on Wilderness Point. The small parcel of land had been a gift to her and her husband from one of the 'old money' families because Sean Sullivan landscaped their property and took care of their house when they were not on the island, and Kathleen had become very close with the family through teaching their children sailing every summer. It was an astoundingly generous gift and Kathleen and Sean never stopped thanking the family that had given it to them. The Sullivans built themselves a small cottage on the parcel. It was hidden behind a stand of trees but had a great view of the Atlantic Ocean.

Meg's grandfather Sean had died before she was born and Nanny Sullivan lived in the beautiful cottage by herself. Shay always said that she hated the thought of her mother living all alone on the water, but Nanny would have it no other way; she had built the house by hand along with her husband and had raised Shay in it, so she would never leave.

The Sullivans called their house *Tír na nÓg* (pronounced *teer na noog*), after the Irish mythological Island of the Young. Legend has it that in the far off mists to the west of Ireland, a magical island exists where the fairies live and you never grow old. When the Sullivans first sailed to Fishers Island, they were so amazed at how much it looked like Ireland that Sean was convinced it had to be the legendary *Tír na nÓg*. This was one of the reasons Nanny so easily convinced him to move to the island.

The Sullivans had lived a charmed existence on Fishers Island from the moment they landed. Summers were filled with clam bakes and sunsets and, although they did not see much of each other during the day, they made up for it when the weather got cold. When the summer residents of Fishers Island left for their "regular" houses, the Sullivans looked forward to nights spent around the fire reading and telling each other stories.

It really was a magical place and they lived happily there, but even the spell of their own *Tír na nÓg* could not save Sean from the heart attack that stole him from his family one fateful day years past.

When Sean Sullivan passed away, Mark and Shay had just bought *Sweet Haven* and they invited Kathleen to live with them in Mystic. They were worried about her living by herself on an island, and Shay wanted her mother nearer to her. Kathleen politely refused. The cottage held too many dear memories to just abandon it. She also said that, according to the old stories, the moment you set foot off of *Tír na nÓg*, you would shrivel up and die, and she didn't want to chance that happening to her.

Nanny Sullivan was tall with silver hair that was always cut short. She had the presence and demeanor of a queen, and it seemed as though she could look right through you. At the same time, she had a twinkle in her eye that let you know she was not as stuffy as she looked. She was sitting in her usual place, in a rocking chair on the front porch of her small cottage, her legs crossed at the ankles and her hands resting politely on her knees.

"Hello, Murphy clan!" she boomed with a voice that can only come from a life of calling out instructions over the wind.

"Nanny!" the kids shouted as they ran up the dock to her house.

Sean jumped up on her lap and nuzzled his head into his neck, "Would ya look at this lad. He's as handsome as his father and gettin' bigger by the day." She gave him a hug and looked up at Eileen and Meg.

"And how's Eileen?" Nanny had a lilting Irish accent that had softened only a little from living in America so long.

"I'm good, Nanny, real busy as usual. I have a big dance competition next week and we just found out that my soccer team is going to play in a tournament."

"That's wonderful, dear," Nanny patted Eileen on her shoulder. "Now, Shay, take the wee one from me so I can grab a hold of the birthday girl." Shay picked up a squirming and now unhappy Sean from his grandmother's lap and Nanny pulled a reluctant Meg towards her.

"Ahh, look at ya. As beautiful as a Connemara sunrise, and I think you may have grown since the last I saw ya."

"Nanny," blushed Meg, "I was here two days ago and am just the same."

"No, Meg. I'd say yer definitely a smidge taller and a tad wiser. I watched ya bring the boat between the point and the rock and from the way ya were piloting the *Muirín* in this heavy wind, I'd say yer the finest sailor in these waters. How's my birthday girl?"

"I'm fine, Nanny" said Meg.

"Oh! Just fine, are ya?"

"Just fine," said Meg with a yawn. "I'm a little tired 'cause I didn't get much sleep last night."

"Well, isn't that funny. Neither did I." She looked around at the family. "It was the strangest thing. Around midnight, I was sound asleep and was woken by the loudest crash. I thought a plane from the airstrip had smashed into me front room. I got up and looked around the house, but there was nothing."

"Oh, my God, Nanny! That is exactly what happened to me last night, too." Meg got right in front of her and looked into her grey eyes, "Finn and I thought that a tree had fallen on our house. We looked around, but there was nothing."

Mark chimed in, "I found her outside with the dog around midnight, and she was talking pretty excitedly about a big crash she heard."

"How strange is that?" said Shay. "Both you and Meg heard a loud crash at the same time and in two different places."

Nanny Sullivan pursed her lips and frowned as if she had recalled something bad and repeated, "Strange indeed… a crash… a crash… " Suddenly her face softened as she gave up trying to remember. She said to Meg, "No granddaughter of mine can be 'just fine' on her birthday." She got up from her chair and grabbed Meg by the shoulders. "Tired or not, it's time to celebrate. Ya only turn eleven once."

Just before they entered the cottage, Nanny paused and looked down at Meg. It looked as though she had remembered what she was trying to recall just a minute earlier. She held her pointer finger in the air near her temple and took a breath like she was about to speak, but instead gave Meg a strange smile and continued inside. Meg returned the smile but she couldn't help but wonder what her grandmother was going to say before stopping herself.

6

The Gift

Just inside the door of *Tír na nÓg* was a sort of all-purpose room that served as a living room, dining room, and kitchen. The windows faced the sea and the fireplace was always lit. Nanny had a couple of bricks of Irish turf burning brightly on the fire.

A few years back, Shay had found a distributor of turf in America and had purchased some for Nanny, to give her a treat from her home country. Because Ireland is not heavily forested, there is little natural wood available to burn in fireplaces. For centuries the Irish have been cutting bricks of peat bog and drying them out to use later as fuel for their fires. Peat is composed of decaying plants that have been compressed for thousands of years in wetland bogs. These bogs are then carefully trenched and cut into bricks using a *slane*, a spade-like tool with a flat blade that has a wing on one side that allows two edges of the bog to be cut at the same time. The dried turf burns longer and more evenly than wood and produces a sweet-smelling smoke. When Nanny Sullivan lit a brick of turf for the first time since leaving Ireland, the scent brought tears to her eyes. In fact, Nanny was so overwhelmed with memories of her home that she immediately signed up for regular deliveries of turf and it was now the only thing she burned in her fireplace. Even blindfolded, it was possible to find Nanny's house on Fishers Island just by following the sweet aroma of a turf fire.

Nanny swung the tea kettle that was hanging from a hinged bar and chain over the fire. She sat down in a chair that faced the fireplace and windows looking out to sea. The kids sat on the floor in front of Nanny as Shay grabbed tea cups and plates from the cupboard. No visit to Nanny's would be complete without a cup of tea and, of course, cookies. As the cups were handed out, Nanny Sullivan looked at Meg with a big smile and began.

"Now, as ya know, our family has been in love with the sea as far and as long as we have been around. It's in our blood. When I was a child on the Island, I learned to swim before I walked 'cause there was always a chance of being dropped overboard, as we traveled everywhere by boat." Nanny winked and the kids laughed. "Most fishermen on our island didn't want to learn to swim because they would rather go right under the water if their boat sank, but we were always different. Me father was a fisherman by choice, not necessity; he came from a long line of sea captains." Nanny held her head up high with pride.

"You see, a ship captain spent his life at sea and was rarely at home. My father loved my mother so much that he couldn't stand to be away from her on the long voyages, so he gave up being a captain of a ship for becoming a fisherman with a *currach*. It was a simpler life and much harder but he was able to be with his family every night, and that, he said, was worth more gold than any ship could hold."

Meg loved to listen to her grandmother tell tales of the old country. She never missed a chance to come out with her mom when she came to check on Nanny.

"But a captain he was, one of the best in Ireland. He knew how to sail by the stars and he taught all of his seafaring knowledge to his daughter—me,—and this is what he taught me with."

Nanny reached into the drawer of the side table next to her and took out a beautiful, ornate-looking metal object. She held it up for a moment for everybody to see and then handed it to Meg. It looked like one of those old-fashioned pocket watches but it was just a little larger and very heavy for its size. It was made of brass or bronze, was well worn from use, and had etchings all over the surface of beautiful Celtic knotwork, along with all sorts of strange, stylized creatures. On the face, in the middle of all the artistic etchings, was a strange letter that Meg didn't recognize. It kind of looked like the number 5 but the top of the letter was long like a T. There was a hinge on one side and a latch on the other.

"Go ahead…Open it, Meg," Nanny urged.

Meg carefully pushed the latch open to reveal a set of instruments, all in the same brassy metal, ingeniously hidden inside of the cover. These instruments were covered in more etchings and words in what looked to Meg like Gaelic. One of the instruments was flat with discs and levers, another looked like a sundial when folded out, and yet another had a compass in the middle. Each instrument was covered with numbers, words, and beautiful artwork. It was, without a doubt, one of the most beautiful things Meg had ever held in her hands. Holding it as if it was a sacred relic, she looked up at her grandmother with a quizzical look.

"It's an astronomical compendium, a sort of Swiss army knife of ancient mariner's instruments. With it you can calculate time, latitude, longitude, the tides, and the movement of the stars. Your family has used this tool to travel the world by sea for generations, and I'm hoping your mom will teach you how to use it, because it's yours now." Nanny Sullivan looked down at Meg. She was beaming with pride.

"Oh, Nanny… I can't…I just can't take this from you. It is priceless," Meg said.

"Ya must, Meg. I will never travel away from this place, and your mother has followed in the footsteps of my father and become a fisherman. Eileen will be a movie star someday," said Nanny, winking at Meg's sister, "so it is up to *you* to travel the world and follow in the family tradition of being a great sea captain."

"Oh, Mom!" said Shay "The compendium. Really? It should be in a museum somewhere, not in the care of a little girl."

"Mommy is right, Nanny. This is a treasure, and I just can't take this from you," Meg said, trying to hand the compendium back to her grandmother.

Nanny looked around the room with her sternest, queenly stare. She was clearly upset with their words and was just about to speak when little Sean jumped on her lap yelling "Treasure!" breaking the tension. At that, they all had a laugh. Nanny held her little grandson, smiled, and looked again at her family. The kindly twinkle had returned to her eyes, but she was still very serious.

"This *treasure*," she said, tickling Sean, "has been handed down in my family for ages, each time to the next, great, seafaring child. It would have been my brother's..." Upon mentioning her brother, Nanny made the sign of the cross, touching her finger first to her head, then to her chest, then to her left shoulder, then her right shoulder, "... had he not been lost at sea at eighteen years of age, God rest his soul. After losing his son, my father didn't even want to give it to me, for fear of losing his only other child to a watery grave. But I swam out to his currach one day and forced him to teach me its secrets." Tears welled up in her eyes, and she added, "It no more belongs in a museum than I and it is as much a part of our family as the blood that runs in your veins."

Meg took the gold chain that held the compendium and put it around her neck, tears streaming down her cheeks. "I am honored to carry on the family tradition, Nanny."

At that moment, the radio on Nanny Sullivan's counter crackled to life.

"Coast Guard station to *Tír na nÓg*. Kathleen or Shay, are you there?"

7

A Death in the Family

"Shay, are you at your mother's?" came the familiar voice over the radio.

"*Tír na nÓg* to Coast Guard station. Yes, John, I am at my mother's. What's up?"

"We just got back from Race Rock Light and there was no woman out there. Are you sure you saw someone there?"

"Of course we did, John, or we would not have called it in. She was an older woman with white hair sitting on the sea wall, the whole family saw her. Did you see a kayaker on the water anywhere near Race Point?"

"There was no one on Race Rock Light and no boaters on the water, Shay. No one but you or your mother would be out near The Race on such a windy day with the tide going out. You must have seen that ghost from the TV show, over." With the last response they heard laughter in the background.

"A woman with white hair out on Race Rock Light?" Nanny said, looking more serious. "Ya didn't tell me about this."

"I haven't had the chance to tell you yet. As we were coming up towards Race Rock Light, we saw an older woman sitting on the sea wall. We figured she was one of those crazy ghost hunters that had paddled out there, because she was in a long, grey dress just sitting on the wall."

"And crying!" blurted Meg, surprising her family. "I heard her crying as we approached."

"I already told you that was the rigging singing, Margaret Grace," Shay said sternly.

"No it wasn't. It was just like the crash last night. You didn't believe me about that, but Nanny heard it also." Meg pleaded, "Nanny, as we neared Race Rock Light, I heard a woman wailing and crying on the wind… And then we saw her on the wall. She was bent over and combing her hair and…and…crying. I know it was her."

"Meg, Sweet Pea, you are overtired and emotional and you are letting your imagination run away with you," said Mark, trying to ease the situation.

There was an awkward silence and then everyone noticed that Nanny Sullivan was crying.

"Nanny, what's wrong" said Eileen.

"He's dead," she said, wiping tears from her eyes. "It all makes sense now … Everything. I knew I had heard that crash before and the '*shee* confirms it."

"Mom, who is dead? 'Shee?' Do you mean banshee? What are you talking about? I think we all need to calm down, take a deep breath, and pull ourselves together," said Shay.

Eileen grabbed her grandmother's hand. "Who's dead, Nanny?"

"My father."

"Your father. Mom, I didn't even know I had any living grandparents… And now you say one is dead."

Nanny stared into the fire, motionless for what seemed to be an eternity. She then spoke, not lifting her gaze from the burning turf. "I was a little girl, only about Meg's age... I was playing out in the fields. It was a lovely day... I was watching a beautiful white cow that I had never seen before, walking along the *lough* when a storm came in out of nowhere off the Atlantic. Me father and brother were out fishing as usual and me mother came out to the field where I was and rushed the two of us into the cottage for shelter.

"The storm was fierce and the wind cut through the walls of our cottage like they weren't even there. All afternoon me mother and I waited and prayed that me father and brother would walk through the door in their oilskins, but they never came... It was a long and heart-wracking day, but I had fallen asleep somehow." She paused and took a sip of her tea.

"In the middle of the night, there was a loud and terrible crash that shook the house to its foundation, that woke me from me sleep. With the storm blowin' outside, I thought something had been thrown onto our little cottage, but me mother knew what had happened." The recollection of the crash made Nanny's hand tremble, causing her tea cup to clink in its saucer.

"Me mother told me that stormy night how the old families are watched over by the spirits, and when someone from an old family passes to the other side, the fairies knock the houses of their kin to let them know. When me mother heard the crash, she knew right then and there that me father and brother were dead. She was crying and inconsolable for the rest of the night.

"The next morning the storm had passed and we went out to the shore to look for the bodies." Nanny Sullivan looked up from the fire and said to them, "First we heard her, for her *keen* is known all across the land and sea. The melodious and sad wail was coming from the banshee mourning the death of her kin. We walked towards the shore and we saw her on the rocks in the distance, in a grey cloak, crying and wailing as she combed her white hair. Me mother and I rushed towards the 'shee but when we reached the rocks it was gone. Then, miracle upon miracles, we found me father on the shore, clinging to his life along with an oar from his missing currach, but me brother was nowhere to be found." Nanny reached for her handkerchief to dry her tears again. "We carried me father home and nursed him back to health, but we never recovered me brother's body."

Meg looked up from Nanny and then over to her mother, who looked like a deer in headlights. Nanny cleared her throat and continued, "Me father was never the same after. By day he sailed around the ocean and at night he walked the shore, always searching for his lost son. I stayed by his side as much as I could, but he would not let me go to sea with him no matter how much I begged. One day I got so fed up with being left behind that I swam out to him as he was pulling away in his boat and he had no choice but to bring me on board. He begrudgingly took me along. We sailed along the coast, from island to island looking for the remains of me brother. The next day he didn't say a word to me but waited at the door of our cottage for me to follow when he left, so I knew he wanted me to come along. We searched all over and spent a lot of time on the Atlantic. A family friend lent us a sailboat and we pushed out our search even further. It was on these searches that eventually he taught me the skills of the sea and navigation. One night, after a long voyage, he gave me the compendium that he had taught me with." Nanny pointed to the object in Meg's hands.

"Day after day, week after week, month after month, we searched for my brother's body. If it weren't for the kindness of our neighbors we would have starved because me father had stopped fishing. Don't get me wrong. I missed my brother, too, but you must move on at some point. After months of searching I begged him to come back to the world of the living and laugh with his wife and daughter. But a death at sea is hard to accept, for you never can say goodbye to the mortal remains, and me father was heartbroken from losing his only son. I was young then and didn't understand everything, and I was also very headstrong. I could not get over me father's refusal to let go. I stopped going out with him on his searches and we ended up fighting all the time. So when I turned eighteen, I hopped on a ship and left him and me mother behind."

Shay was dumbstruck. "Mom, I had no idea. Why haven't you told me any of this before?" she said.

"Hard memories are best left behind so they don't weigh ya down," said Nanny with a scowl.

There was an awkward silence.

"I have grandparents," Shay wondered aloud.

"You *had* them. I kept in touch with me mother by letter, as there were no phones on Inishbofin back then. She knew all about ya, Shay, but I never again talked with me father. It was a bad situation. He didn't even let me know that me mother had passed on when she did. I had to learn that from a neighbor that knew our family. They were the ones who wrote to tell me she was gone, not him."

There was deep pain and sorrow in Nanny's eyes and she looked down at Meg. "So now, with that crash and you seeing the banshee, I know that me father has left this world. The spirits know—they look after our family and are never wrong. I'll make a call into his neighbor to go and check on him."

No one moved or said a word. They were all staring at the fire and letting this new information settle. After a minute Meg got up and hugged her grandmother, and the family soon followed her in a big group hug. After, everyone sat back down and sipped their tea in silence. Finally Nanny Sullivan looked out of her window to the ocean and, out of nowhere, said, "Looks like a storm is brewin'. You better get back on the *Muirín* and head home."

"Nanny, there is not a cloud in the sky," Eileen challenged, after looking out the same window and not seeing anything.

"I wouldn't mess with your Nanny, Eileen. She has never been wrong about the weather."

Everyone helped wash and put away the dishes, and the Murphys were soon saying their goodbyes and walking out the door of *Tír na nÓg*. On their way out Nanny grabbed Meg while the family continued without them. Before she could say a word, Meg told her "I promise I will guard our compendium forever, Nanny."

"I know ya will, dear. But remember, it's just a tool. What you have inside of you is a greater treasure than that old piece of metal."

Meg turned to leave and paused her glance at the horizon on the Atlantic in front of her. For a second, she thought she saw dark clouds looming. But just as fast as she saw them, they were gone, replaced by the clear, blue sky meeting the rolling ocean waves. She looked back at her grandmother, who again gave her the same strange smile she did when they first walked into the cottage. Nanny gave her a hug and said, "Happy birthday, Margaret *Grace*," emphasizing her middle name in a weird way. Meg walked to the sailboat wondering what had just happened.

8

Happy Birthday

It was a somber sail. Everyone was withdrawn and in their own world. Meg let her mom take the helm for the ride back. She needed it. Meg had seated herself up near the bow, staring at the compendium and processing everything that had happened: the crash, banshees, unknown great grandparents, and great uncles lost at sea—it was a lot for an eleven-year-old girl to take in. Meg knew her mother was having a hard time with it all, too, because she noticed the telltales luffing much more than they normally would with Shay captaining.

They sailed up the Atlantic side of Fishers Island. The wind had died down a bit, enough to make the sailing a little more relaxing, even if not enough to slow them down. By the time they rounded the eastern tip of the island and were heading back towards Connecticut, the sea had done its job and everyone was a little more at ease. Sean made up a song and was singing from his seat. At that everyone smiled and started talking again.

"I loved the old stories from Ireland growing up but I never thought I would live one… a banshee… The vision of that woman is burned into my brain right now… I have never heard about the crash before," Mark said.

"*Banshee* is Irish for *fairy woman*. *Bean,* pronounced *ban,* meaning *woman*, and *sídh*, pronounced *she*, meaning *fairy*. They are said to be caretakers of the noble Gaelic race in general, or anyone with a *Mac* or an *O* before their name.

> *By Mac and O*
> *You'll always know,*
> *True Irishmen they say.*
> *But if they lack*
> *The O and Mac,*
> *No Irishmen are they.'*

It's a silly old rhyme, but Nanny used to say it when she would tell me stories of the banshee."

"But Nanny is a Sullivan," Eileen said.

"Her maiden name is O'Flaherty, Eileen."

"Oh. So banshees guard families?" Meg asked.

"Yes, the old Irish families, and in the folk tales banshees also guarded the fairy gifts given to those families. Some families had the gift of music; some had the gift of art."

"What about the gift of the sea and navigation?" interrupted Meg.

"I'm not so sure about that. Navigation is more of a learned skill than a gift. But we do have a love of the sea don't we?" She winked at Meg. "A banshee wails a sad and sweet cry called a *keen*, which is copied by women all over Ireland at funerals and wakes. Ooohhhhh, woooohhhh," Shay did her best banshee keen.

"I'm scared, Mom," admitted Meg. "I can't get the vision of her out of my head either, or that wail."

"Banshees aren't scary things," she smiled and tilted her head to the side. "They are friends of the family they guard.

They supposedly walked the earth with the family, possibly even being a long-dead member. The banshee keen is one of sadness, because she no can no longer follow her friend. As a banshee, she is stuck between this world and the otherworld."

"How do you know so much about this stuff, Mom?" asked Eileen.

"Nanny and your grandfather, God rest him, told me all of the Irish legends and stories when I was little. In the winter we would sit in the big room around a roaring fire and tell stories and read books until the spring came again. It was like going to Ireland every year when the weather got cold. Kings and queens, fairies and ghosts, battles and cattle raids were my entertainment when I was your age, Meg."

"I want to hear more," said Meg.

"Me too," added Eileen.

"All right." A smile crossed Shay's face. "I'll tell you all the tale of an Irish princess who sailed the seas with a magic compendium she received on her eleventh birthday…"

"Aw, Mom!" complained Meg.

They all had a laugh, and then listened to Shay make up a fairy tale about Meg as they sailed towards the restaurant in Stonington.

*   *   *

The village of Mystic is part of the larger town of Stonington, which is situated on a harbor that was also once a very busy seaport. On the docks at the tip of the peninsula that makes Stonington Borough, as the locals call the old part of town, there is a restaurant where the Murphys held all their celebrations—birthdays, anniversaries, hallmark holidays. It did not take much for Shay and Mark to come up with a reason to go there. Just a short ride from their house by car or by boat, it was their favorite place to go to eat. The Murphys were always given a prime table, on a corner of the deck that extended out over the water.

The sun was shining brightly and the temperature was warm for October. The deck was filled with people soaking up the sun and fresh air on the last of the nice days before shutting themselves up for the winter. The owner of the restaurant stopped by their table, as always, to say hello and talk to Shay about the next shipment of her scallops. When the business discussion with Shay was done, he took their order for dinner. Mark and Shay ordered steaks. The owner always kidded them about coming to a seafood restaurant to order beef, but that is what they always had. Meg's parents said they spent enough time around seafood at work so they never wanted to have it for dinner.

Meg, on the other hand, loved seafood. She had the most wonderful seared scallops (her mom's, of course) and a big plate of French fries. Their dinner was finished off with a chocolate cake brought out by the wait staff as they sang "Happy Birthday" to Meg. The whole crowd on the deck helped with the singing. Then Shay went down to the *Muirín* and came back carrying gift bags.

Meg's birthday present from her dad was a book by her favorite author. She loved to read and already had quite a large library of books that she kept in a chest in her room. Reading was a way for Meg to go to places she could never dream of and live stories that could only be possible in an author's imagination. She was not like most kids her age who spent time zoned out in front of a TV or computer. Meg read most anything her parents let her, in both hardcopy and on her electronic reader, which was last year's birthday present. Her e-reader was full of books from antiquity, which she downloaded at first because they were free. Soon enough, however, Meg found herself truly enjoying the classics.

Meg's mom gave her something she had been waiting a long time for: scuba lessons. You were not allowed to learn to scuba dive until you were ten, and even then you were only allowed to learn under a certified diving professional. Shay did not want to get Meg diving under water too early, so she had always promised that she would let her scuba dive when she turned eleven. Meg had been snorkeling for as long as she could remember, but swimming around the surface of the water with a big plastic tube in her mouth never was as cool to her as diving deep for hours with a tank. She had been very much looking forward to reaching the age of eleven so she would finally be able to go down and dive with her mom. The crazy thing was, even though Meg finally got what she had been waiting for forever, all she could think about at the moment was what had occurred earlier that day and the compendium that hung around her neck.

Meg stared down at the oversized ornament. On her small frame, it looked a bit silly. "Mom, what is this letter on the front?"

"It's a *G* in Gaelic script."

"What does it stand for?"

"I don't know, and have always wondered that myself. Your Nanny would always smile and change the subject whenever I asked her. Maybe it's the initial of one of our ancestors or maybe she doesn't know."

Meg took her eyes off the compendium and looked out on the water. The setting sun was shimmering on the surface of Fishers Island Sound making the island look as if it was magically floating out in the distance. She looked at her family and her gifts and decided that it had been a good birthday, even with all of the strange events.

They left the restaurant just after the sun set, sailing back home in the dusk, and were almost back to "Sweet Haven" when the weather suddenly changed. Clouds came in from nowhere and it started to rain, just as Nanny had predicted. The wind picked up and thunder clapped in the distance as they pulled the boat up to their dock. No one bothered to get into the foul weather gear Shay had packed; they just tied the boat up and ran into the house through the downpour. By the time everyone got in the door, they were soaking wet and tired from the day's events. They all retreated to their rooms and went to sleep, not noticing that the answering machine on the kitchen counter was blinking.

9

Want to Go Somewhere?

Meg woke up the next morning a little groggy from a night of heavy dreaming. Although she had had many dreams during the night, she remembered only one. *She was swimming under water and below her in the sea bed she could see the compendium resting in the sand. She was swimming as hard as she could but there was a strong current pushing her away from her birthday present and she was unable to reach it. The shining brassy object eventually disappeared into the dark water in front of her and she was heartbroken for losing it.* After the dream Meg shot up in bed, reaching out from her covers in panic, only to be comforted upon seeing the compendium on the nightstand where she had left it.

Meg dragged herself out of bed and took the compendium in her hands. She went to put it on but decided that it was too big for her to wear all the time, so she placed it at the bottom of her old toy chest that was now filled with books. She went downstairs for breakfast.

Everyone except Meg's sister was at home. They were all very busy when Meg reached the kitchen. She walked in unnoticed, trying to figure out what was going on. Her mom was on the phone and her father was on the computer. Eileen was probably at soccer practice and Sean was in his high chair crying for attention. Meg made herself a bowl of cereal, poured a glass of orange juice, and sat down at the table to listen to the conversation that was going on around her.

"I know I promised you a delivery by next week, but a family matter has come up and I won't be able to get them to you until the week after… I know you're desperate, but as you know, I'm a one-woman show, so if I'm not around there are no scallops…Try the distributor…I know they're not as good, but you are just going to have to wait."

Meg's mom was obviously doing business, but what has happened that she's unable to make her deliveries? And her dad, who normally by this time would have been long gone and out on his boat, was staring at the computer screen with a pencil in one hand and a mouse in the other, clicking and writing at the same time.

Shay got off the phone and asked, "Mark, what do you have for me?"

"Tomorrow from Logan and…" The phone rang and Shay held up her hand to stop him while she answered the phone.

"Mark, it's your sister."

He picked up the phone. "Hey, Molly, thanks for calling me back… Yeah, mostly Sean, just for a week… I can't stop fishing, and Eileen can take care of herself, so I need help with Sean." There was a long pause. "She's actually going with her mother."

Mostly Sean? She's actually going with her mother? What, exactly, was going on?

Just then, Shay, who had taken up Mark's place at the computer, noticed Meg at the table.

"Morning, honey. Make yourself some breakfast. I have some exciting news to tell you," she said, not looking up from the screen.

Meg shook her head as she looked down at her half-finished bowl of cereal. She turned to Sean and said, "Parents!"

Her dad hung up the phone, "Okay, so Molly is going to come up, stay here at the house, watch Sean while I'm out, and help with Eileen. She's happy to spend some quality girly time with her."

"I want to spend girly time with Aunt Molly too!" chimed in Meg.

"Oh, Meg, I don't think you will care about time with Molly when you hear what your mom has to tell you."

Shay walked away from the computer and stood next to Mark. "I got JFK tonight, and a much better price, Mark. Hi, Meg. Want to go somewhere special with me?"

"Um, I guess. Do I have a choice?"

Shay told Meg about the message that had been left on their answering machine. Nanny Sullivan had called the house last night while they were at dinner and confirmed that her father—Meg's great grandfather—had indeed just died back in Ireland. His neighbor had found him after Nanny called to ask them to check, and arrangements were being made for his funeral. Nanny was too frail to fly and Shay really wanted to go to Ireland to represent the family at her grandfather's funeral. She decided it would be a great trip to take Meg on to learn about their family history together.

"Ireland? Really?" Meg was thrilled with the idea but still taken aback at the suddenness of it all.

"We are flying out tonight. So you need to get back upstairs and pack a bag for a week."

"What about Eileen? Why isn't she coming?"

"I asked her. But she has her big dance competition next week, and a soccer tournament, so she wanted to stay home. Plus," Shay raised one eyebrow, "Inishbofin is an island reachable only by ferry, and you know how we feel about motorboats, so I chartered us a sailboat to get there. It will be a good chance for me to teach you how to use the compendium while seeing the place where we came from. It will be great!"

"Are you forgetting something?" asked Meg.

"I don't think so."

"I'm in school. What about school?"

"I've already emailed your teachers. They've given me all of your school work for the next week, and you are going to do a presentation on our trip when you get back, for extra credit." Shay saw the worried look on Meg's face. "Don't worry. You'll have plenty of time to do the work on the plane."

"Extra credit. Great," said Meg patronizingly "You really thought of everything, didn't you." She thought about it a little longer and said, "Well, a trip to Ireland for Halloween sounds pretty good to me."

"Oh no! I totally forgot about Halloween! Mark, you are going to have to take pictures of Sean and Eileen trick or treating, and maybe you should cancel our annual party."

"Don't worry. I'll take plenty of pictures. Just because you two get to have fun in Ireland doesn't mean we can't have fun back here." Mark did a little dance, which made them laugh. "If you guys want to catch that plane, you'd better get a move on and get packed."

Meg and Shay dashed up the stairs leaving Mark and little Sean on their own. Meg realized she had not seen her dog yet that morning and yelled "Fiiiinn. Finn, come here boy." The dog appeared at her door, tail wagging. "Okay, boy, listen. I'm going away for a week so you are going to stay in Daddy's room," she scratched the dog behind the ears and he looked up at her with sad eyes. Finn was a shaggy, white mutt they had saved from the pound a few years back. When she was little Meg had shown an interest in every dog she saw. Since her sister was so busy and out of the house a lot, her parents decided to get Meg a playmate. Shay named the new dog Finn, which meant *white* in Gaelic. And since then Meg and Finn had been inseparable from the moment he joined the Murphy family.

Finn sat and watched Meg as she packed her bag. She opened her toy chest and picked up the compendium. Carefully wrapping her special gift in a tee shirt, she placed it in an inside pocket of the book bag that she was going to take with her on the trip.

"How's it going in there?" her mom called out from down the hall.

"Fine, Mom," Meg yelled back. "I still can't believe we are doing this."

Meg heard her mother shuffling down the hall. Shay stepped in the door and handed her a little blue booklet.

"What's that?"

"It's your passport. Surprise! We were actually planning to go to the Caribbean for Christmas this year, but it will have to wait for next year, I guess. Don't tell your sister, though. It'll have to be our little secret."

Meg crossed her heart and continued packing, her sad dog at her feet.

10

First Flight

Aunt Molly showed up at the house just as they finished packing. She helped Meg get her bags downstairs. "How exciting! You get your first airplane ride and trip out of the country at the same time."

"I know! I still can't believe it," replied Meg.

It was true. Meg's family had never taken her on an airplane before because they rarely took long vacations. The surprise Christmas trip she just found out about would have been their first. According to her father, living on the water was a vacation all year long. Whenever they did go somewhere, it was always just short trips. And, Meg's parents could never leave their businesses for a long trip, because they both operated their fishing boats by themselves and worked all of the time.

This never bothered the Murphy kids because they really did live a great life. During the summer Meg was constantly swimming and snorkeling around the island or reading on the dock. When she got bored with that, she could always spend the day sailing with her mom, reading on the *Muirín* while Shay dove. She had fun on the water and in the sun every day. Meg's tan never went away, even in the winter. Eileen, as far as Meg knew, never had a problem with not going away either. She was so into her sports and dancing that she was usually out of the house before Meg got up in the morning. Meg loved her family and her home, and didn't know anything else, so vacations were not something to miss.

Eileen was dropped off from practice as everyone was outside loading up the car. She ran up to them and gave her mother a big hug. She said to Meg, "I sure am jealous. Mom and Dad have never taken me anywhere on a plane." Meg's eyes twinkled remembering the secret she now shared with her mother, that they would have been taking a trip if this funeral had not come up.

Shay looked down at Meg to make sure she was silent on the now-canceled Christmas trip and said to Eileen, "I promise you that we will take a vacation to someplace far away very soon. Right, Mark?" Their father put his arm around Eileen's shoulder, gave her a squeeze, and nodded an affirmative, "Yup."

Shay grabbed little Sean who was already squirming to get out of Aunt Molly's arms. She gave him a big hug and kiss. He didn't know what was going on, but said, "Bye, bye, Momma," and ran off towards the house with Molly in tow. Mark, Shay, and Meg got in the car for the two and a half hour drive to New York City. They waved goodbye to Eileen and Finn who were standing on the porch as they pulled away.

A few years back, the Murphy family had sailed down Long Island Sound and spent the night in New York on one of their short family trips. Meg thought it was the most amazing place she had ever seen. They walked around the city under the massive buildings and bright lights. Everything was huge and buzzing, like a hive of bees. She was awed by the amount of people constantly walking the streets, seemingly at all hours. While she was in the midst of it all, Meg wondered how the people who lived in New York City could put up with the constant noise and being separated from nature. Sure, they had Central Park and trees lined some of the streets, but everything around the city was encased in concrete and stone.

At home, Meg woke up to the sounds of the shoreline, with birds and frogs and bugs singing all day and night. The honking, yelling, and din of the city were alien to her, and she had spent the one night they stayed in New York looking out the hotel window and not being able to sleep a wink. Thankfully, the next day they got back on their boat and sailed around the Statue of Liberty and Ellis Island, returning to the water where she felt most at home.

Remembering that trip, Meg started to think about what it must have been like for Nanny Sullivan to leave her family at such a young age. She pictured her on the bow of a ship entering New York Harbor and seeing Lady Liberty for the first time. She envisioned that the sight would have brought tears to Nanny's eyes.

It was unthinkable to Meg that someone could leave their family forever. At the same time, though, she could not fully grasp the idea of death; nobody in her family had died in her lifetime, other than a couple of goldfish. Meg didn't even know about those until later on, when her sister told her that their parents would just switch out the dead ones for new ones before she realized it. The thought of losing her sister or brother was unimaginable, and her parents, even worse, but it had to take something that tragic to send a young woman from Ireland to never see her family again.

It was hard on Meg to learn that she had a great grandfather one day, only to find out that he was gone the next. The thought of Nanny possibly dying someday was just too much for her to even ponder. Yet, here she was, sitting in a car heading towards an airport to be with her mom for the funeral of her great grandfather. Just then, she realized that she didn't even know his name. His last name was *O'-something*, but she hadn't learned his first name.

"Mom, what's my great grandfather's name?"

"Owen…Owen O'Flaherty."

Owen O'Flaherty. She didn't know any Owens, at least not personally, but there was that cute movie star with the crooked nose.

'Mac and O', something, something Irish they be' What was that rhyme her mom always said? Meg then realized it didn't matter, as she was from Irish royalty and had a banshee following her every move. *At least it wasn't one of those creepy leprechauns.*

Every St. Patrick's Day since she was little, Meg would pour milk into her glass in the morning and it would magically turn green. Her parents said it was the sneaky Leprechaun playing tricks on her family as usual on March 17, Ireland's Patron Saint's holiday. They would search around the house and try to find the little spirit but they were never able to find him. At least the green milk didn't taste bad.

Meg looked out the car window. She saw they were only at New Haven. *Still quite a while to go.*

She grabbed her backpack that held her school work for the week and the compendium. Carefully, she pulled the compendium out and unwrapped it to look at it again. It was just so beautiful.

As Meg fingered the compendium, she observed it was oblong, but not egg-shaped, and about four inches long on the widest side, about the size of her palm. It was nearly an inch thick, with an interlacing Celtic knotwork band around the perimeter. The lines of the knot wove over and under themselves in a never-ending sequence.

Celtic knotwork art, her mom had told her, was used by monks in Ireland to adorn the manuscripts they transcribed. The most beautiful example of this is the famous *Book of Kells* held at Trinity College in Dublin. The geometric designs were influenced by the Middle Eastern art of the time, but they came to have a life of their own in the hands of the Irish monks who created ever larger and more complex knots that could be traced from beginning to end as one never-ending line. It has been said that the knots represent the eternity of life, love, or nature, but no one is really sure if they had a deeper meaning or were only decorative. Meg always had fun following them from any point on the knot, all around the twists and turns, over and under, back to where she started— it was almost meditative.

The front of the compendium, as Meg's mom had explained at her birthday dinner, had a Gaelic script letter *G*, which looked nothing like the way she read or wrote the letter. *Grace...* In the back of her mind, Meg heard Nanny saying her middle name like she did when they left her yesterday. Looking at the letter closely, Meg traced it with her finger and she heard it again. *Grace*. The more she looked at it, the more she liked the way the letter *G* looked in Gaelic script. It was surrounded by animals and beasts all interwoven together just like the knotwork on the side of the instrument.

The other side of the compendium had a woman's face with flowing, curly hair that radiated from her head like the rays of the sun. Unlike the decoration on the front side, which was etched on the surface, the reverse was like the face on a coin, almost three-dimensional. The woman's face was emotionless and her eyes stared straight ahead.

Meg let the long chain slide through her fingers. It was attached to the compendium by a clasp that was etched with scrolls. At the top edge of the compendium was a small, round ball that, when snapped into a small hole in the clasp, held the compendium closed. There was a hinge on the bottom of the compendium that allowed each instrument to fold open freely while still remaining attached.

Meg pushed the latch back and opened the compendium. The first instrument she saw was a magnetic directional compass in the center surrounded by an engraving of a square. Engraved along the edges of the square were the numbers *3*, *6*, *9*, and *12*. These numbers were repeated two times per side, on all four sides of the square. An engraved circle of boxes and tick marks surrounded the square. The tick marks were numbered in increments of ten, and went from *10* to *360*, which Meg knew were the degrees of a circle. Attached to the compass in the center were two arms that had little fobs at each end that folded up. One of the fobs had a hole and the other had a point. From sailing, Meg knew that you looked through the hole to the point and compared your direction with the direction of the compass needle that always pointed north to figure out the course you were traveling.

The second instrument was a round, hand-held sundial that folded out on its own hinges. The edges of the sundial were also engraved with tick marks and numbers, and a quadrant was attached in the middle of it.

The third instrument was not an instrument at all, but more like a page in metal. The page contained a list of words in Gaelic, and after each word there were two numbers. The reverse side of this page had more inscribed words, but these were lined up in columns. The words were so small that Meg was unable to make anything out on top of everything being in another language.

The last instrument was comprised of a series of thin, overlapping discs with all sorts of geometrical markings. Each disc could be turned in a circle like a dial. There was a hole offset in the center disc that Meg realized showed the phases of the moon when she turned it. She also recognized the symbols of the twelve zodiac signs aligned around the disc, along with more numbers and tick marks. One of the discs was a frame of arcs and points that revealed etched outlines and dots below it. Meg turned this disc and saw that the lines beneath sometimes matched up with the points of the arcs, although she did not know what this represented.

The back plate of the compendium had another movable arm attached to the center with fobs that folded out and numerical tick marks all around the perimeter.

The compendium was as complicated as it was beautiful. The engravings and inscriptions were starkly black from rubbed-in dirt, while the bronze was smooth and shiny. Meg's mom had taught her basic navigation with a compass and charts, but she had no idea how this piece of art could help her sail a ship. Looking at the different instruments with their complex markings, Meg was intrigued. She couldn't wait to learn how to use them.

She studied her gift a while longer, folding out the leaves and turning the dials and gizmos first one way then the other, then finally closed it. To think that several generations of her family had held this tool in their hands and used it to sail the seas sent chills up Meg's spine. She then shuddered at the thought that the compendium was also held by the now-dead Owen O'Flaherty, the man she was about to fly over the Atlantic Ocean to see for the first time, at his funeral! She wrapped her treasure back up in the tee shirt and replaced it securely in her bag, vowing she would never let it out of her sight.

The drive went by more quickly than she had expected and they were soon pulling their car into John F. Kennedy International Airport in New York City. After unloading at the curb in front of the terminal, Meg said goodbye to her father. It was weird leaving her dad behind. Meg had never spent a significant amount of time alone with just one parent. Days spent with her mom on the sailboat were always balanced with snuggle time with her dad at night. As Mark pulled away and they walked into the terminal, Meg already missed him more than she ever thought possible.

After Meg and Shay got their tickets, they had some dinner in an airport restaurant that was jam-packed with people. Most were happy and looking forward to their trips, but Meg also noticed the business travelers who were unimpressed with air travel, sitting with straight faces as they typed away at computers or looked at their cell phones.

Meg was excited to be traveling ... sort of. But she was also a bit scared to go on an airplane. The idea of floating on air in what looked like a big, long metal can was not natural to her. Boats on water made sense, and besides, the air was for birds. They walked around the terminal, amid all of the air travelers. Meg started to get anxious about getting on the plane. Her mother must have noticed Meg's apprehension and was extra comforting and even hugged her a few times which was very unlike Shay. Meg told her mom she was a little scared of flying. Shay told her she had nothing to worry about, and hugged her tightly again. They bought some magazines to read while they were waiting and found a space on a bench near the door to their plane. A short time later, they handed the flight attendant their tickets and walked down an enclosed ramp to the long metal can with wings.

When the flight attendant pulled the door closed, Meg grabbed Shay's hand and squeezed it tight.

"I'm scared, Mommy."

Shay looked down at Meg and kissed her on the top of her head. "You have nothing to worry about, honey. Remember, our family is protected by the fairies and they won't let anything happen to us, especially since we're traveling back home to Ireland." The look in her mother's eyes reassured her and the thought of magical protection was comforting, but Meg found herself looking out the window for the banshee just in case. Meg did not see it anywhere and the plane took off without a hitch.

Soon they were flying over the water that Meg had spent her whole life on. For as long as she could, she watched from her window as they flew up the east coast of America. Below, the yellow lights of the towns and cities shining in the night were pretty, and Meg's nerves were calmed by the monotonous droning of the jet engines. She had no interest in watching the in-flight movie, and fell asleep when the dark ocean was all she could see out of the small airplane window.

11

The Auld Sod

Meg's first flight lasted a total of six hours and fifteen minutes. The sudden movement of the plane approaching Shannon Airport woke her. It was morning, and a vast, motionless white ocean stretched out as far as she could see. It was a beautiful and peaceful sight. The plane made another turn and she was looking straight down on the fluffy white clouds that looked as though they would be the most comfortable bed in the world. Meg felt the downward motion of the plane in her stomach but the fear and anxiety of the previous day were gone.

The airplane descended and all Meg could see out the window was bright, white light. Her mother was paying close attention to a Welcome-to-Ireland video playing on the screen above them. Meg was more fascinated with flying through the clouds. The sinking feeling in her stomach let her know that they were getting closer to landing. The misty white beyond the wings opened up for just a moment to reveal green fields below Again and again the blank white was replaced with living green, but only for a short period of time before fading into the mist again. When the airplane was finally flying below the cloud cover Meg saw field after field of grass, each separated by grey stone walls. Everything was so green. Meg had heard that Ireland was forty shades of green, but until she saw it for herself she had no idea what that meant.

After the airplane touched down, everyone onboard applauded. Meg was not sure if they were clapping for a good landing or just the fact that they were finally in Ireland. It didn't matter. Her first airplane ride was uneventful and it didn't even feel that long because she had slept through most of it.

The door of the aircraft was opened to a cloudy day. A light rain was landing softly on the tarmac. Stepping out into the Irish air Meg sensed that she was home—not home in Connecticut, but really, truly home, that place where you know you belong. It was a strange feeling, but one she felt down deep in her being. Meg walked with her mother up the ramp to the terminal and soon enough they passed through customs, received a stamp in their passports, and walked out and set foot on the land their family had come from.

Because it was early morning, other than the passengers from their flight, there were not many people milling about. Shay had obtained all the transportation information they needed on the internet before they left Connecticut, including maps and schedules, and she led Meg right to a bus stop outside of the terminal. The plan for the day was to take a bus to Galway City. There, they would pick up their charter boat and sail up the coast to Inishbofin Island which, according to her mom, was not far from Galway.

While they were waiting for the bus to arrive, Shay looked down to Meg and said, "Isn't this amazing, Meg? Isn't it just so beautiful?"

Meg looked around and took a deep breath. The air was damp but not heavy. To her, it had the smell of living. That was the only way Meg could describe it: living, green. "As soon as the door opened it felt like home."

"I felt the same way the first time I came here," replied Shay.

The first time, Meg thought, but before she could ask her mom to clarify the statement, a bus pulled up from the opposite direction she was expecting surprising her. It was on the wrong side of the street! But that was not the only difference. The bus itself was backwards as far as she was concerned, the driver was on the right side, and the door they entered was on the left. As they loaded up their bags Meg made a mental note to look the other way when crossing the street. The bus left the airport and was soon whizzing past the green fields of Ireland.

"I'm glad we're on a bus, Meg. I definitely would've had a hard time getting used to driving on the left!" Shay said as they made their way towards Galway.

Meg nodded in agreement. Her mother was an amazing boat captain but when it came to driving things with wheels it was a different story.

The highway they traveled, called the M18, was nicely paved and very clean. It wove its way through the Irish countryside that consisted mostly of fields in every shade of green. These fields were divided by tumbled stone walls. The landscape showed every undulation of the earth as far as the eye could see, and the fields and stone walls combined to make it look like a patchwork quilt. The thing that struck Meg as odd was that there were no trees, at least not as many as she would see at home. Back in Connecticut you couldn't go anywhere that wasn't heavily wooded, but here in Ireland the trees were few and far between. Nanny burning turf in her fireplace made more sense to her now that she saw the forestless landscape for herself.

Not only were the roads they traveled and the towns they stopped in different from what Meg was used to, she also noticed that the houses in Ireland were not like those in Connecticut either. She was used to multi-story colonials with shingled or clapboard siding, with a shingled roof and painted in all sorts of colors. Irish houses, Meg noted, were mostly one story, covered in stucco or stone, and grey. A couple of the houses she saw had straw-covered roofs. Her mother told her that those were thatched roofs, which is an old type of roofing that layered straw instead of shingles to shed water off the dwelling. The bus traveled through the lovely landscape, every so often passing the ruins of a castle or an ancient building. The landscape was like a story book setting to Meg. Images of knights on horses galloping by and princesses trapped in castles flew through her mind as they rolled up the M18. She never had these types of thoughts when driving around the countryside back home.

There were just a few other passengers on the bus. Meg figured it had to be because it was early morning. Seated across the aisle from them was a little old woman who must have noticed they were tourists. She smiled and said, "Visiting Ireland for the first time?"

"Yes," replied Meg. "This is my first time out of America."

"You're from the States, are ya? What part?"

"Mystic, Connecticut," they said in unison.

"I have family in Boston. Is that near ya?"

"Kind of. We are a little south of Boston."

The woman paused for a second then asked Shay, "It is Galway ye'r heading to?"

"Yes. But we are only just stopping there before we head to Inishbofin Island. That's where our family is from."

The woman raised her chin in acknowledgement of the name "Ah, yes. I've never been there meself, but the islands off the coast of Galway are lovely. Have ya relatives there?"

"Yes and no," answered Shay. "We are here for the funeral of my grandfather. I never met him and, as far as I know, we are his only kin."

The woman crossed herself, "May God rest his soul."

Shay continued the conversation with the woman across the aisle while Meg looked back out the window at the beautiful countryside. It was still raining, but only passing showers. Every so often, the sun light would find its way through the scattered clouds and shine down like a spotlight, often creating a rainbow. Meg called each one out for her mother to take a look. Shay would look for just a short time and then go back to the conversation she was having, clearly not as impressed with the magical imagery as Meg. On this short trip there were more rainbows than she had seen in her whole life.

All of the road signs in Ireland were in both Irish and English. They stopped in towns with names like Crusheen, Ardrahan, and Oranmore—names as foreign to Meg as any she had ever heard. A couple of times she had to ask her mom how the strange words were pronounced—sometimes the Irish names were exact matches and sometimes they were a far cry from the English names. She was able to read *Croisín* and its English version *Crusheen* on one sign without too much trouble. Her mother explained that the letter *S* in Irish was pronounced *SH* when followed by a vowel, like her brother's name Sean. The English Oranmore is *Órán Mór* in Irish, and Ardrahan, *Árd Raithin*. Meg saw a sign for Dublin, the capitol of Ireland, and its Irish version *Baile Átha Cliath*, which did not resemble the English Dublin at all.

The rural landscape soon changed into the urban expanse of Galway City, and the fields were replaced with streets and buildings. Meg saw the sign for the city and recognized the Irish version of Galway, *Gaillimh* (pronounced *gall-yiv*. The *mh* makes a *V* sound in Irish), as one of the words on the compendium. Galway, the third largest city in Ireland, lies on the River Corrib that empties into Galway Bay on the west coast of Ireland. Shay told Meg that Galway is a center of the arts and the Irish language.

It was late morning when they got off the bus in Kennedy Memorial Park, or Eyre Square, in the center of the city. There were street performers scattered about, all very entertaining. The last time Meg saw street performers was when they were in New York City. Shay pointed out a bust of John F. Kennedy, thirty-fifth President of the United States. The square is officially named for JFK, although most people in Galway still call it by its old name, Eyre Square. After walking around for a short time they decided they were hungry and looked for a place to eat. They walked through the park which was on a slight hill. At the top of the hill, the girls found a fast food restaurant and had some lunch. Shay had brought along an Ireland guide book and read aloud the history of the city while they ate. Amazingly enough, they were enjoying Papa John's pizza. American fast food is everywhere!

"Galway was founded by the King of Connacht in 1124," Shay read. "It was originally a fort but grew into a settlement and a walled city soon afterwards… Ireland was invaded by the Normans in 1169 and the city fell into their hands… The Normans who stayed assimilated into the Irish culture and eventually became, as they say, 'more Irish than the Irish themselves.' The tribes of Galway, as the Norman ruling families came to be known, eventually gained total control over the city and were granted mayoral status by the English Crown. This led to bad relations with the surrounding Irish and, get this Meg," Shay said, pointing to the book, "the tribes of Galway had posted a sign on the west gate of the city that read 'From the ferocious O'Flaherty's, may God protect us.'"

"That's us, Mom! Cool!"

Shay continued, "The native Irish were allowed only limited access into the city and there was a by-law saying 'Neither O' nor Mac shall strutte nor swagger through the streets of Galway' without permission. The city was run by an oligarchy."

Meg interrupted, "What's an oligarchy?"

"An oligarchy is a form of power through a small group of people." Shay continued, "The city was run by an oligarchy of fourteen merchant families consisting of twelve Norman and two Irish. These were the 'tribes' of Galway."

"Interesting. Mom, how about that O' and Mac thing again, just like the rhyme you told us about the banshee?" Meg asked.

"In Irish *Mac* means *son of* and O' means *grandson of*, or descendant. Back in the old days, people just had a first name, called a *given* name, and would be addressed by their given name with the name of their father."

"So I would be Meg MacMark."

"Actually, your name would be Margaret Ni Murphy, Margaret daughter of the son of Murphy, or something like that. The rules are different for women, but in general, for Irish women the O' is *Ni* and the *Mac* is *Nic*."

"Confusing," said Meg.

"It gets worse. You can also find *Mór* and *Óg* in Irish names meaning *Big* and *Young*, respectively, kind of like the *Jr.* for *Junior* and *Sr.* for *Senior* designations in English, to distinguish a father and son with the same given name. On top of that, there are descriptive names, like, for instance *Padraig Rua*, which means *Patrick with the red hair*. And my favorite, because it could be used for you, is *Beag*, or *little*, which would indicate a person's size or sometimes premature birth. You were premature so you could be *Meg Beag*."

"I like that one. It rhymes… Really, Mom, how do you know all of this stuff? It could not have all come from stories Nanny told you."

"Meg, my mom and dad were immigrants from Ireland and I lived on an island that resembled their country in many ways, so, from an early age I studied anything and everything Irish. I learned the history, the language, and the culture, and was very proud to be an Irish woman. For me, it became a mantle I could put on to overcome my shyness and small size."

"You're not shy, Mom."

"I used to be. And growing up an only child on an island didn't help. But as I learned about Ireland and the Irish, I found I could relate to other kids often by just talking about where my parents came from. I love Ireland. When I was a teenager I even spent a summer here with a cultural program that immersed American students in everything Irish, and I traveled the whole country." Shay's face grew sullen. "It makes me a little sad to think about that now. Had I known I had a grandfather, I could have met him when I was here last." She drifted off for a second, pondering the thought. "But you can't change the past, can you, Meg? Let's finish up and get down to the docks to see the kind of boat we will be sailing up the coast."

They ate the last of their pizza and walked back down the hill through the other side of Eyre Square towards the water. They passed a fountain with a sculpture of rust-colored triangles that looked kind of like sails. It moved her in a way no piece of sculpture had before. It was as though she knew what it represented, even though it was just a bunch of rusty, red triangles.

"What kind of boat did you charter for us, Mom?"

"There is nothing better for these waters than a 'Galway hooker.'"

"A Galway hooker?" said Meg, giggling.

"Get over the name, honey. They are traditional sailing vessels in these parts, kind of like my 'New Haven Sharpie' *Muirín*. Up until the age of powerboats, the hooker was the main kind of boat for carrying cargo on the west coast of Ireland. They fell out of use and were nearly lost to history until some dedicated sailors brought them back. I was lucky enough to find one to charter, but the owner is very protective of it, so we have to sail him out to the Aran Islands to prove we are capable before he'll allow us to take it on our own."

"Sounds like a challenge, but it's nothing the ferocious O'Flahertys can't handle. I wonder, though, why we are ferocious," Meg said with a laugh. Together, they made their way towards the shore.

12

The Red Sails

It was just after noon when Meg and her mother reached the docks where they were meeting Paddy Mullen, owner of the *Cailín Mo Chroí* (pronounced *coleen mo kree*). The harbor was filled with many boats and Meg tried to figure out which one they would be taking. At the entrance to the pier they saw a rotund man leaning on a metal fence puffing away on a pipe.

"Paddy?" asked Shay.

"Aren't we all over here?" came the reply from the man, not even looking up from his pipe. *Paddy* was a derogatory term for an Irishman.

"Sorry. I'm looking for Paddy Mullen."

"Oh." He looked up with a smile and a nod, "Well, you've found him, haven't ya?"

Paddy Mullen was a middle-aged man with graying hair showing from under his tweed cap. He was overweight and had a ruddy, red complexion.

"Hi. I'm Shay Murphy. We spoke on the phone yesterday."

"Well, that's grand. And who's the lovely girl?"

"This is my daughter Meg."

He looked at Shay and Meg and furrowed his brow while puffing on his pipe "So, I'm asking myself why two Yank ladies are looking to hire my boat for a week, on this chilly October day."

"We are sailing up to Inishbofin Island to arrange for my grandfather's funeral," Shay replied.

"I'm sorry about your grandfather... Inishbofin..." He raised his eyebrow before continuing. "You know, it is the twenty-first century. There's a fine ferry service that goes out of Cleggan twice daily to Bofin Island. You can drive up the lovely Connemara coast to get there."

"We are not interested in taking a ferry. I'm a captain and my family has sailed these waters as far back as any. Meg and I want to see the Connemara coastline from the only perspective fitting for O'Flaherty women—from the tiller of a boat." Shay seemed a little bugged by the man's attitude.

"O'Flahertys," he said as he drew another puff of smoke from his pipe. "Why didn't you say so? I should know better than to cross an O'Flaherty. Please, please get on board," he said, pointing to a black sailboat tied up to the pier.

The *Cailín Mo Chroí*, which Paddy later told them meant *girl of my heart*, was about twenty-feet long with a hull as black as night. The black color came from the fact that it was covered in pitch, or tar, which was the traditional way to waterproof a boat in Ireland. She had a single mast and an upswept prow with a long bowsprit to which two foresails were attached. When they hoisted the sails Meg was surprised to see that they were a dark red instead of the usual white. The rusty-red triangles in the fountain in Eyre Square made a lot more sense to her now.

"Why are the sails red, Paddy?" Meg asked.

"The reddish-brown sails go back to the calico sails that were used at the time these boats were originally made. T'would'nt be a hooker without the red sails. In fact, the only Galway hooker that is allowed to use white sails around here belongs to the King of Claddagh."

"Claddagh? Like the rings?" said Meg. She was referring to the traditional Irish ring that was formed by two hands rounded to clasp a crowned heart.

"Claddagh's the small fishing village just across the river from the Spanish Arch in Galway City. Sure, it's famous for the ring now, but it has always been a fishing village. The fishermen of Claddagh elect a King to lead 'em and make the big decisions, ya know. He sails a hooker with white sails. We may see him on the way out."

"What are the rules on Claddagh rings again, Mom?"

"If you wear the ring on your right hand with the heart pointing out, it means you are looking for love. If it is on your right hand with the heart pointing in, you are in a relationship, and if worn on the left hand with the heart pointing in, it means you are married."

"It's like an old-fashioned relationship status indicator," Meg said, looking down at Paddy's left hand. She saw that it bore a gold Claddagh with the heart turned in.

Paddy gave the girls a lesson in the boat's design and rigging and told them that traditionally there were four classes of Galway hooker: the *Bád Mór* (big boat), the *Leathbhád* (half boat), the *Gleoiteog*, and the *Púcán*. The first two were larger and used for hauling cargo, mostly turf. The last two were used for fishing. The *Cailín Mo Chroí* was a small *Gleoiteog* that had been outfitted with a cabin to be used as a pleasure boat. Paddy was a successful businessman and had commissioned her to be built by young, formerly unemployed, Irish-speaking boat builders who were keeping the tradition of Galway boat building alive. Paddy had her christened the *Cailín Mo Chroí* after the pet name he called his wife.

Meg and Shay impressed Paddy with how quickly they learned the boat. They sailed west out of Galway Harbour under the watchful eye of Paddy, who sat in the bow looking back at them while puffing away on his pipe. Following the coast of Connemara, in Galway Bay made famous by song, they saw more fields of green in between the stone walls that seemed to be everywhere in Ireland. The coastline was much rockier than Connecticut's and the conditions more challenging than Meg had imagined they would be. The wind was blowing hard and they had to stay extra alert to the sea and how the boat handled it.

Things were tense. Paddy sitting in the front of the boat not saying a word wasn't helping matters. Meg could tell her mom was a little nervous. She barked orders as if Meg didn't know what she was doing. It didn't bother Meg. Her mom was the captain, and when they were on the water she wasn't her daughter, she was the first mate. The pressure of performing well on an unfamiliar sailboat in a heavy wind and choppy sea was turning this short October sail into something more like work, not like the typical fall sailing they do at home.

Sailing on Long Island Sound in October was the best time of year. There were fewer boats out and the water was still very warm from the summer sun. The water on the Irish side of the Atlantic was a little cooler than they were used to; it was around fifty degrees. But like home, the fall here also saw much less boat traffic than in the busy summer. Although Meg kept her eyes peeled for the white sails of the King of Claddagh's sailboat, the only boat they saw was the ferry heading in the same direction as they were, to the Aran Islands.

When the grey islands rose on the horizon, Paddy turned his head forward, easing the tension and allowing the girls to enjoy the sail.

13

The Big Island

Three Aran Islands lie just outside of Galway Bay in the Atlantic Ocean: Inisheer, Inishmaan, and Inishmore, named in size from smallest to largest. Shay said that they are populated by hardy people who have kept the Irish language as their primary language, and who have made their living by fishing the waters of the Atlantic along with growing crops on the land. Meg, Shay, and Paddy were headed to Inishmore, the big island, to spend the night and, if they passed the test of seamanship, hopefully to drop off Paddy.

The trip would usually take about an hour by sail, but Paddy demanded that they first do a few maneuvers in the bay and he then had them go around the Atlantic side of the island to see how they handled the boat in rough waters. Nanny wasn't kidding when she talked about learning to sail on the harsh west coast of Ireland. Along with the dreary weather, the wind was very hard and the waves rough.

Inishmore is basically a big rock, as are its sister islands. On the Atlantic side of the island, sheer limestone cliffs are battered by endless waves. Meg did her best to not stop and stare at the sight of the looming walls of stone as they sailed past. The bluffs of Block Island back home in America were the only things Meg could compare to the cliffs of Inishmore, but the Mohegan Bluffs rose up gradually where these cliffs shot straight up from the ocean and there was no beach at the bottom.

The ocean waves rolled and crashed around them and the wind blew in a steady gale, but the girls handled the boat expertly the whole trip. As they pulled into the sheltered harbor on the opposite side of the island, Paddy got up from his seat in the bow and joined them, again, saying nothing. But his smile showed he was seemingly satisfied of their ability to take care of his boat.

It was late afternoon and jet lag started to set in on Meg as they tied up to the pier and gathered their bags. She let out a big yawn.

"Don't fall asleep, honey. If you take a nap now you will never adjust to the time difference," Shay commanded.

"But I'm sooo tired."

"We'll have to stay busy until nightfall to hold off on falling asleep too early."

On their way up from the docks Paddy led them past a beautifully carved Celtic cross, to a place called The American Bar. It was a yellow, two-story building with a mural that showed New York City and the Statue of Liberty with a Galway hooker sailing by. Meg loved the mural, especially the touch of the Galway hooker. Paddy told them that a local man fell in love with an American girl and never left the spot where he said goodbye to her. He eventually built a bar and restaurant named after the place where his lost love came from. They walked into a dark bar and everyone in the pub looked up when they entered.

Shay walked up to the bar and ordered two pints of Guinness, one for herself and one for Paddy, and a soda for

Meg. Although the pub was busy it was not packed, and there were two musicians playing Irish music in the corner of the room.

"It's nice here at this time of year," Paddy said. "Most of the tourists are gone and ya can actually find a seat in the pub. I wouldn't come here normally, but I wanted ye Yanks to feel at home."

"We know all about tourists. We live in a popular tourist destination in America. Thanks for the gesture, but we didn't come this far to be in an American bar," said Shay.

"Sorry about that, Mrs. Murphy," Paddy said, a bit taken aback by Shay's words. He took a sip from his drink then looked at Meg and Shay with a twinkle in his eye. "I have to say, you are definitely O'Flaherty girls by the way you handled me boat. I was a little nervous when we met on the dock, seeing as you were two wee lasses, but I'd say you can handle her better than meself. You're fine sailors, the both of ya."

"My mother learned how to sail as a child on Inishbofin and taught me everything she knows."

"Me too" proudly added Meg, with a big yawn.

"Stay with me, Meg," Shay said, patting her on the shoulder as a reminder to stay awake.

"I have charts in the cabin for the whole west coast, but ya probably don't need 'em, do ya? Bein' O'Flahertys and all."

"We are not magicians, just good sailors, and we will definitely use the charts. Does this mean we can have her?"

"She's yours for the week."

While Paddy and Shay exchanged details of the boat charter, Meg diverted her attention to the people around her. She could always pick out the tourists with their backpacks and cameras back home, and there were only a few here.

Seated next to where Meg, Shay, and Paddy were sitting two old men, hunched over their Guinnesses and deep in conversation. Meg tried to listen in, but they were speaking in Irish, which sounded like no language Meg had ever heard. Other than a few words here and there, she had never actually heard Irish spoken. There were a lot of throaty, hocking sounds in the language. The men also talked in very hushed tones, almost mumbling, and barely cracking their lips open to talk. The strange thing was that even though they were speaking with words she did not know, Meg recognized the intonations and rhythm of the way they spoke. Her Nanny talked the exact same way, and Paddy did, too. His mumbled English, which Meg sometimes had a hard time understanding on the boat ride over, had the same cadence of the two old men speaking in Irish.

After his drink was finished, Paddy stood up and shook Shay's hand. "Well, good day to ya, and take good care of my girl." He nodded towards the boat tied up to the pier. "I'll see ya's in a week." The two old men Meg had been listening to looked up when Paddy spoke. They gave him a nod in recognition, and on his way out, Paddy gave each a pat on the back. "I'm tired, Mom. When can we go to sleep?" Meg said with a big yawn.

"Not yet. We have to wait until it's night. I have an idea, Meg. Let's figure out what time sunset is."

"Why don't we just ask someone?"

"I have an even better idea. Hand me the compendium."

Meg reached into her backpack, pulled out the compendium, and handed it to her mom. Up until this point, Meg had sort of forgotten about it. Shay opened it to the instrument with the dials and engravings.

"This one is called a *volvelle*. It's a tool that allows us to figure out how long daytime is based upon the date and our latitude. We first need our coordinates which are on this leaf," she said flipping to the next tool in the compendium and pointing to the list of words with numbers, "These are names of ports with their latitudes and longitudes."

She pointed to *Gaillimh* on the list.

"Galway," Meg said.

"Yes, Meg! So, we turn this dial to the latitude," Shay said, turning one disc, "this dial to the longitude," turning another, "and now we can move this dial to the middle of Scorpio because today's date is October 28." She turned the dial to one of the marks of the Zodiac engraved in the brass. "Now, if we look at the sun," she said, pointing to an engraved sun, "we see that today it rises at around eight." Shay indicated a pointer on top of the sun pointing to an inscribed numeral *8*. On the flip side she showed a moon that had a pointer directed at a numeral *6*. "And it sets around six. So we have a couple hours to sightsee before we'll finally be able to get some sleep."

Meg nodded but, because she was so tired, she was not fully following all the movements her mom made on the compendium. Shay folded the compendium back up and handed it to Meg, who put it back away in her backpack. They walked out of the pub and back out onto the road just outside. Just coming out of the dark pub helped Meg wake up. They looked around and saw bikes for rent. They also saw vans for hire and horse and buggy rides available. They decided on a horse and trap, as it is called in Ireland, to go up the large hill to the Neolithic fort of Dun Aengus. The trap driver was an old man who welcomed them by saying, "*Fáilte roimh chách, mo chairde, go Inis Mór.* Welcome, my friends, to Inishmore. My name is Thomas, and your tour guide today will be the beautiful Aran pony, Johnny Cash." Meg and her mom both giggled at the joke, and the pony was soon clip-clopping its way up the narrow road.

Dún Aonghasa, as it is spelled in Irish, is perched high up on one of the cliffs they had sailed past earlier that day. The fort was built of loose stones piled one on top of another. They formed concentric walls that were almost twelve feet thick in places, and that ended abruptly at the edge of the cliff. It was if the walls were full circles at some point in the past, and half of them had fallen into the ocean. They were allowed to walk right up to the edge of the cliff, and they did. Three hundred feet below them they saw the waves of the Atlantic crashing into the cliff. The view was both dizzying and commanding at the same time—it was truly awesome. As they stood at the edge, the wind was whipping them. They soon backed off because it was a little scary. Meg and Shay also spent some time looking at the ruins and a while later returned to the horse and trap for the ride back down the hill.

All around them they saw tiny parcels of farmland divided by stone walls. The fields here were just like the ones they had been seeing all day on the mainland, only much smaller. The trap driver explained to them how the islanders had converted the inhospitable rock of the island into farmland by layering sand and seaweed to make fertile beds for growing crops. Meg was astounded that people could create farmland out of rock to survive. After just a short time on Inishmore, Meg could see that the Aran Islands were an amazing place.

In just her first day in Ireland, Meg had traveled by bus, boat, and horse and trap, and she had seen in this one day more wonderful things than she had seen in her whole life. The wind blew her hair as she looked out to her surroundings. *This is where I came from and this is where I belong,* she thought. The cold air kept her awake, but she could feel all the hours they lost flying over the ocean creeping up on her like a warm blanket.

By the time they sat down to dinner, Meg was so exhausted that, a couple of times, her mother had to save her from falling asleep into her plate of food. After dinner, they finally checked into a small bed and breakfast hotel. They were shown their room, and within minutes Meg blissfully fell asleep.

14

Sailing Home

Meg was so tired she could have slept for a couple of days; the fresh island air and the exhausting schedule they had kept the day before could have easily seen to that. But they had to get to Inishbofin. When Meg's mom woke her up at the crack of dawn, Meg's head was still foggy with a new dream from the night past: She was riding in a motorboat at high speed, and she did not feel comfortable because of her vow to ride only in sailboats. The motorboat was racing over wave after wave, and water was crashing all over her. She had to get somewhere and it had to be quickly, but she was woken up before she knew where she was going in the dream. Just dreaming about riding on a motorboat bugged Meg the entire time she was getting dressed and gathering her things for the day ahead.

After getting packed up, Meg and her mom went downstairs to a breakfast of fried eggs, potatoes, and something called a *rasher*, what the woman at the Bed and Breakfast said was supposed to be bacon but looked more like ham. Meg tried to make a sandwich out of the rasher but it was just not the same as her favorite breakfast sandwich at home. Irish food was something she was going to have to get used to. After breakfast mother and daughter made their way down to the pier and boarded the *Cailín Mo Chroí*.

The sun was out and the sea was a little calmer than it had been when they came in the day before. Shay and Meg cast off from the pier. They raised the mainsail and sailed their way towards their ancestral home. The course they charted up the Connemara coast would get them to Inishbofin before the day was over, depending on the wind, which did not seem to be a problem in these waters. Shay called out orders to Meg in a much nicer way than she did the previous day, and Meg carried them out with precision.

"Hoist the foresail." Meg trotted up the deck and pulled on the line attached to the red sail until it fluttered and then filled with wind.

"Let out that line." By the time her mom called out that order, Meg had already noticed that the sail needed to be let out and was loosening the line attached to the long wood pole that held the bottom of the sail.

"Watch the spar."

"Prepare to tack." Meg dropped to the deck getting ready for her mom to swing the boat and its sails for the wind to come from the other direction.

"Tack ho!" Shay turned the tiller and the spar and sail swung gently over her.

Meg loved to watch her mom sail. Shay was so confident and commanding at the helm of a sailboat that, even when they took friends out on the *Muirín* back home, they all often just naturally followed whatever she said. Meg's mom was that way on land, as well, and was the center of attention wherever they went. Her confidence and demeanor outshone her short stature. Shay was everything Meg wanted to be, but wasn't—at least not yet.

Meg had never been one of the popular girls at school. Her small size had led her to being very shy around other kids her age, and she found it hard to make friends. She didn't dance like her sister and, because she sometimes felt short of breath, had never got into sports, two activities that helped Eileen gain a lot of friends. Meg could never find anyone who would just play by the water and pretend the same way she did. Her days were spent in her own little world with her imagination always keeping her company.

Like most other little girls, there was a time when Meg wanted nothing more than to be a princess. When out playing in the surf, she was always the Little Mermaid, splashing her feet together like a fin. Her mom said she had no fear of the water when they first took her to a beach, and would have walked right out into the sound and drowned if they hadn't stopped her. As a toddler, whenever Meg took a bath, she would always try to stick her face in the water, a habit that drove her parents crazy. Meg was convinced she could breathe underwater like her princess hero Ariel.

After Meg had outgrown the princess stage, some days she pretended to be a famous sea explorer combing the ocean floor for new kinds of fish. When she was out on her mom's boat she was always a pirate captain sailing to find buried treasure. Shay and Mark found it unusual that Meg was always by herself, so they often tried to pair her up with some of their friends' daughters and sons. Meg tried to play with them, but no lasting friendship ever bloomed as a result. The problem was that the other kids never wanted to do things Meg's way, and Meg was stubborn and only wanted things her way.

Compared to her sister Eileen, the social butterfly who was always on the go, Meg was a hermit. She never wanted to leave the vicinity of her home and its surroundings. Of course, Meg had to go to school like all kids do. In fact, school was kind of easy for Meg because she always loved to read. Meg's big problem was doing her homework. After coming home from a long day at school, especially when it was nice out, she went straight to the docks or to the shore to play. When it wasn't nice outside, she stayed up in her room snuggled up with Finn and reading.

While Meg's test scores in school were always good, her grades suffered because her after-school activities took up the time she really should have spent doing school work, so she lost homework points almost every day. Her parents never punished her for her bad grades because they knew she was smart, but they often told her how disappointed they were with her school work. The last thing Meg wanted to do was disappoint her parents, but since they were usually still out on their boats when she got home from school, she found it hard to sit down and concentrate on her homework when there were so many other worlds to discover on her own in a book or outside in her backyard. The course Meg plotted was her own, but like most sailing trips, she had to either follow the way the wind carried her or beat against it in the direction she wanted, and she almost always chose the latter.

As they sailed up the coast, Meg and Shay marveled at the strange beauty of the west coast of Ireland. Off the side of the boat they saw sweeping vistas of green fields perched upon cliffs and sandy beaches. Meg wondered if those beaches ever saw sunbathers because of the spotty weather in Ireland. The land was rocky and so was the shoreline, and there were numerous islands and coves scattered everywhere. It would have been rough sailing in these waters without the charts that showed the subsurface rocks everywhere. At times, the landscape before them looked more like the moon than a place on earth because it was so barren and rocky. They viewed land and water scenery that few tourists ever got to experience, and they knew it. In spite of the challenging sea conditions, Meg and Shay were really enjoying sailing past peaceful fields and the weather-beaten coastline.

The boat rose and fell on great swells of water, and Meg thought that the Atlantic Ocean seemed harsher on this side than it did at home. Sure, Meg had encountered some big waves sailing with her mom past Montauk, New York, but they were not as powerful as the ones she was experiencing here. The sailing was hard and their skill was being challenged with every swell.

They had been sailing hard for a few hours when Shay decided that they should take a break and have some lunch. She steered the boat into a sheltered cove on the lee side of a rocky island sheltered from the wind and dropped anchor. They had packed a couple of sandwiches and, while they ate, Shay told Meg more about this part of Ireland where their family was from.

In the seventeenth century, England made numerous attempts to conquer Ireland, outlawing the customs and language of the Irish. Ireland was divided into four provinces: Ulster in the north, Leinster in the east, Munster in the south, and Connacht in the west. During one invasion of the

English under Oliver Cromwell, now considered a cruel and tyrannical leader, the English adopted his "to hell or Connacht" saying for use when subduing the Irish. Cromwell's campaign of subjugation drove the Irish from the fertile farmland of the other provinces to the rocky land of the west. But even there the Irish were not safe. A murderous crusade raged across the land, with punitive laws being enforced on the mainland. As a consequence, the Irish were forced to escape to the islands to preserve the language and the culture they loved.

In the long term, even after Ireland gained its independence from England in the 1920s, the damage to the language had been done, with only a small number of Irish people still using Irish as their primary language. The number of people who continue to speak mainly Irish grows smaller each year. Irish, or Gaelic, as it is also called, can still be heard in tiny pockets in the country and scattered along the coast in places like the Aran Islands. These areas are called the *Gaeltacht* (pronounced *gale-takt*). Although learning Irish is mandatory in all schools in Ireland, and the language will never completely die, its time as a common language has long passed.

"Mom, I want to learn Irish to keep it from dying."

"That is very noble, Meg. You know, since I only know just a little, maybe we can learn it together."

"I would really love that, Mom."

The thought of spending more time with her mother made Meg very happy. They finished their lunch and were soon sailing fast up the coast. They passed another rocky cliff with a scraggily green field on top, and Meg imagined how hard it must have been for people to live on such inhospitable land. Just the thought of a family needing a way to grow crops and figuring how to "build" farmland with seaweed and sand on top of rocks made her proud of the kind of people who were her family's ancestors.

"What did Nanny tell you about our family's history?"

"Not much, actually. I've learned more this week than I have in my entire life. She would just say that we came from the islands off the west coast of Ireland and were once great sea captains."

"You would have to be great sea captains to sail these waters, huh, Mom"

"This is definitely not Fishers Island Sound, Meg," her mother said with a smile.

Looking at the coast of Connacht from the rocking boat, Meg's mind drifted off. She was daydreaming of sea captains and ships and escaping from invaders to save a heritage. Her existence seemed so childish up to this point; all she had ever done was play and read. Meg thought of the compendium that was hanging around her neck and had a newfound goal for her life. It was up to her to save the family legacy, become a great sea captain, and to travel the world. It was an easy dream to have at this moment, sailing up an unknown shore in a sailboat with billowing red sails.

They were enjoying the sail on a broad reach, almost running with the wind. Suddenly, the wind changed direction. In an instant, the sheets back-winded and the boom that held the main sail swung violently across the hooker throwing the *Cailín Mo Chroí* on its side. Shay was caught off guard, as she was not fully used to the boat, and did not release the lines in time to stop it. Like a rag doll, Meg was thrown overboard into the cold water.

"Meg!" she heard her mom scream.

The shock of the cold water hit Meg like a wall, taking her breath away. She fought to catch her breath and righted herself in the water. The ocean swells were huge, and she struggled to swim back towards the boat, "Mommy!"

Meg was heaved up and down, water crashing over her, but her lifejacket kept her head above the water. She swam as hard as she could, but despite all of her efforts the boat kept getting farther and farther away.

Swim, Meg, swim, she thought to herself. Meg saw her mom swing the boat around to come back towards her, but it seemed that she was caught in a current opposite the wind. The current swept her out to sea while the wind pushed the hooker and her mom away from her.

In between the waves she could see the boat and also the cliffs that she had seen earlier. But with every rise and fall of the waves, they became smaller. Meg was breathing so hard and was so cold that she could not think straight.

All right, Meg, fifty-degree water should give me about thirty minutes before hypothermia…, or is it fifteen minutes? As she thrashed against the massive swells, Meg tried to remember the boating safety course she had taken when she was nine. No matter how hard she swam, she was unable to change how fast she was drifting away from land and her mother.

In what seemed to be an eternity, she finally stopped swimming to see if she could get her bearings. When she looked up she could no longer see the cliffs on the shore. Her inability to see land scared her to death, but she easily made the red sails out from the grey-green ocean and swam harder.

Come on, Mom. Get that boat moving. Meg could see that Shay was forced to tack the boat back and forth against the wind to follow the current that was dragging Meg. The wind was strong, and Shay was tacking quickly, but the distance between Meg and the boat grew by the minute. Unlike the boat, Meg had no wind resistance and her little body was being carried away with the strong current at a rapid pace.

Between swells, when she was at the bottom of a wave, fear overtook her. But then, on the up swell, she would get a glimpse of red triangles in the distance, and felt hope. The roar of the waves filled her ears with white noise. Up and down, comforted and terrorized, wave after wave, she agonizingly watched the sails shrink from the peaks of water, until finally, after emerging from the bottom of a large swell, she could no longer see the boat.

THIS CAN'T BE HAPPENING! Meg was overcome with terror as she went down into the next valley of water. She swam as hard as she could to get to the top of the next wave, but all she saw in front of her was the heaving ocean.

Meg was seized by the idea of never again seeing her family. Her strokes against the current slowed, she began to cry out loud. *This was impossible. How could this have happened? If only she hadn't been daydreaming and was paying attention to what the boat was doing.* Meg looked up at the sky above her, too tired to swim. Her struggle against the sea had completely exhausted her and she was losing consciousness.

Meg's last thought was of Nanny's brother being lost at sea. Then she felt something push hard against her.

15

The Aftermath

"Meg, honey, please wake up."

Meg heard her mother's voice. Her head was spinning and she was in a thick fog. Then it all started to come back to her. Meg remembered being in the water and freezing cold, and that she had just lost sight of the boat, but she was now warm and dry, and smelled a familiar smell in the air: burning turf.

"Are we at Nanny's?" Meg said in a daze. She opened her eyes and didn't recognize where she was. The room around her was small and dark and she noticed the turf fire burning in a fireplace.

"Oh, thank goodness!" her mom exclaimed, hugging her. "I was worried sick about you." Tears welled up in her eyes. Shay held onto Meg for what seemed an eternity, but the feel of being in her mother's arms after such a frightening experience was just what Meg needed.

"Where are we?" Meg asked.

"We are at Nanny's house. Well, the one she grew up in on Inishbofin."

"Huh?" Meg was confused.

Shay told Meg how she thought she had lost her forever. She tried to get the sailboat back to Meg, but the current carried her away too quickly. When Meg disappeared out of sight, Shay had nearly lost it, thinking her baby was lost at sea. Then Meg suddenly appeared again, apparently in another current that had brought her right back to the boat. Shay said it was the strangest thing she had ever seen in her life. But she didn't care how it happened because she was then able to save her. Meg was unconscious and hypothermic as Shay hauled her into the boat. Shay always carried a hypothermia prevention and management kit when sailing in cold waters, so she immediately got Meg into a heat-reflecting bag, knowing its self-heating liner would help. Shay nursed her with the sails down, and they had drifted for a couple of torturous hours when a passing motor yacht found them and towed them to the island.

"It was lucky for us that a kind man happened to be cruising up the coast to Inishbofin at the same time."

A man stepped out of the shadows. He was older than Meg's mom, and had black hair with specks of grey throughout and a long, drooping grey moustache. Behind his glasses, his tiny dark eyes were cold. He was dressed in jeans and a worn leather jacket, and he had a fedora hat on his head.

"I'm sure glad you're all right," he said. "Your mother was terribly frightened when I reached your boat. We tried to radio for help but could not get through, so we came right to Bofin. You were not that far away when I found you."

Meg gave him a questioning look. He noticed her apprehension and took his hat off. "Bofin is what the locals call the island. The name's Al, Al Woods. You're a lucky little girl," he said in a strange accent that wasn't Irish.

"Thanks. I think," said Meg.

"Mr. Woods towed us here and helped me get you to the only nurse on the island. Thank God he's been here before and he knew right where to go. He stayed here with me all night as I kept watch over you." Meg looked up at the man and smiled.

Shay went to a counter and brought back a cup of tea in a very old, beat-up cup. The smell of the tea overwhelmed Meg's senses and, as she sipped it, she could feel its warmth travel down into her stomach. Mr. Woods walked back into the shadows, sat in a chair by the door, and did not say a word. Shay held Meg's hand after she finished the tea and sat there, just staring at her. In all her life Meg had never seen her mother act this way. It was as if she did not know what to do and, to Meg, Shay was always in control. Finally, Shay looked down at her with big eyes and said, "Oh, Meg, I am so sorry. This is all my fault. We should have just driven up from the airport and taken the ferry here, but instead we had to stick to our ridiculous vow… At a minimum we should have been wearing dry suits. I can't believe I was so stupid."

Meg didn't say anything because she could clearly see that her mother was upset, but in reality she felt just fine. So what if she got a little hypothermic? It was no reason to go against something they both believed in. Thankfully she was swept back to the boat— in her mind she could still feel whatever it was that had pushed her back. They sat there just looking at each other for quite a long time while the fire sizzled in the background. Finally, Meg yawned and her Mother said, "You'd better get some more rest, honey. I need to go into the village to let the nurse know you woke up. I'll bring you back some warm stew, and I want to let Mr. Woods go back to his boat. He has been here a long time." Shay reached down to Meg, brushed her cheek, and gave her another long hug.

"Don't worry, Mommy. I'm okay. It's a good thing you are always prepared and had that hypothermia kit. You have always said it's better to be safe than sorry." Meg looked up and smiled at her mom. "And thank you, Mr. Woods. I sure am glad that you were on the water yesterday."

"As am I, Meg," said Shay returning the smile. "If you think you are okay, honey, I am going to walk Mr. Woods to the village, but I'll be right back."

Meg nodded at her mom and snuggled into the bed. Mr. Woods gave Meg a smile and tipped his cap as he walked out the door with Shay.

Meg looked around her. She was inside a tiny stone-walled cottage, and there was not much around, just a single chair by the fireplace and a few cabinets. On the wall opposite to her was a pair of small windows and a single wood door with a wrought iron handle. Whoever lived here sure didn't take care of the place because it was a mess. Then she recalled it was her Nanny's old house, and realized that this was the place where her great grandfather had died. A chill ran up her spine. She drew the covers over her head and tried to remember what had happened.

She was in the water and thinking about being lost at sea like her great uncle, and she felt something pushing at her back. What in the world had pushed her? Her mom said a current swept her back towards the boat. Could you feel a current pushing you on your back? What could it have been? Whatever it was, it had evidently saved her life.

She heard the door squeak and, despite being frightened, she peeked out from under the covers. A boy about her age entered the cottage. He was wearing a long-sleeved tee shirt and pants with, strangely enough, big rubber boots. Meg saw he had a close-cropped hair cut and, even with the darkness of the cottage, incredibly blue eyes and very red cheeks.

"Excuse me," Meg called out to the boy.

"Ah, yer awake. I saw yer ma leave with The Digger and she asked me to come over and stay wit ya," he said with a deep Irish accent.

"The Digger?"

"Yah, that's what I call yer man who is always digging things up around the island. I tink he's an archeologist like Indiana Jones or something."

"You know about Indiana Jones?"

"Of course I do," he said, offended, "just 'cause I'm on an island doesn't mean I'm backward or something. You Yanks are something else."

"Sorry," said Meg, embarrassed. "What's your name?"

"Dermot Liam Davin. But you can call me Trout."

"Trout?"

"Yeah. Me da likes fly fishing in the rivers when he's not fishing at sea. It's mad. He's a fisherman who likes to fish when he's not fishing. He said when I was little I ran around all of the time and was very hard to catch so he called me Trout and the nickname stuck."

Meg laughed out loud.

"It's good that yer laughing. Your ma thought you were going to die. She said you were nearly swept out to sea."

"I thought I was, too, but something pushed me back."

"Something *pushed* you back?"

"Just before I lost consciousness I felt a hard push on my back. It was the weirdest thing."

"Must have been a selkie," Trout said confidently, spiking Meg's interest.

"A selkie?"

"You don't know 'bout them?" Trout challenged. "They're shape-shifting fairies of the ocean. The selkie looks like a seal but can shed its skin and take human form on land. There are many stories of them and they are all good, but know this, if you ever find clothes on the shore and no one else around," he looked left then right "don't take 'em. They're the enchanted skins of a selkie who is up on land, and if you take 'em, the selkie will not rest until you give 'em back."

Trout looked at her very seriously. "Sometimes a selkie would trick a human into marrying and even have kids with 'em. Then someone in the house would find their seal skin hidden away, by accident like, and the selkie would have to go back to the sea where it came from."

Meg liked this boy.

"But since the selkie still loved their kids and missed 'em, they would come back to play with 'em, but only in their seal form."

"Dermot...err... Trout, I was being swept away by a current and the last thing I felt was something pushing me hard on my back. It did feel kind of like the snout of a seal," Meg said, starting to believe she had been saved by a selkie.

"It had to be a selkie. We always thought The O'Flaherty was searching for a selkie wife. Me da said his wife just disappeared one day and The O'Flaherty was always walking around the shore looking for something. Maybe you have a fairy great grandmother."

The mention of her great grandfather brought Meg back to reality. He was dead and they were here for his funeral.

Trout saw her face change. "I'm sorry. Did I scare ya?"

"No. My mother told me our family is protected by the fairies, but I just remembered that I'm in my dead great grandfather's house."

"Oh yeah, jeeze, I forgot about that. This is the first time I've been in here too," he looked around with a frown on his face.

"Why did you call him The O'Flaherty?"

"He's the last one around here. It's a title like."

"Oh," said Meg and then the door opened and her mother came in with a steaming bowl and a loaf of bread on a tray.

"I better go. Nice to meet ya. I'll see ya's later."

"Thanks, Trout," said Shay, as he walked out the door.

Shay put the tray of food in front of Meg and explained to her that Trout was one of Owen O'Flaherty's neighbor's kids. In fact, Trout's family was the one that Nanny had called to check in on Owen, and they were the ones that found Owen dead. Nanny had grown up with their grandmother and they were the only contact she had on Bofin. Trout had two siblings just like Meg: an older brother Dennis and a younger sister Deirdra.

Trout's father Declan was a lobsterman like Meg's father, but instead of a big diesel boat he used a currach to tend his traps. A currach is a light boat made out of a wooden frame covered, in the old days with skins, but now made with canvas and, like the Galway Hooker, currachs were covered in pitch to keep them waterproof. Meg was told that the small light boats almost floated over the water and were very adept at handling the big swells in this part of the Atlantic. Traditionally they were rowed but many now had an outboard motor attached to the rear.

While Shay was telling Meg all about the neighbors, Meg hungrily ate the stew and almost the whole loaf of bread her mom had brought. Soon after, however, Meg drifted off again into a deep sleep.

16

A Ferry Ride

The sun was shining through the tiny cottage windows when Meg woke up next to her mom in the small bed they shared. She was completely refreshed because, unlike the previous couple of nights, she had had no dreams and slept the whole night through. The turf fire had died at some time during the night and there was a chill in the air. Meg noticed that the fireplace had the same kind of hinged arm for hanging a teakettle that Nanny had in her house back at home, but this one was much larger. There was a large pot next to the fireplace that must have been slung over the fire for cooking and the larger arm must be for handling it.

The floor, like the walls, was made of stone, and it was dirty from not being swept in a long time. Meg looked at the walls. They were white, kind of, but like the floor, they were dirty from years of smoke from the fire and not being cleaned. The whole cottage was in shambles.

Meg's mom woke up shortly after she did and they got dressed and left the cottage. Meg felt completely rested and totally unharmed by her whole ordeal at sea. In fact, she was feeling quite invincible with the fairy protection and all. The wind was blowing hard and the sky was sunny as it had been the day before. The view in all directions was breathtaking. From the door of the cottage Meg saw another island just south of where they were, and to the east she could see the coast of Ireland. The shore was much hillier than what she had seen the day before, and in the distance there were peaks of strangely shaped mountains.

They first walked down to a harbor along a road that was barely paved. Up from the harbor they walked to a fancy hotel. During their walk the weather went back and forth several times between sunny and drizzly. Irish weather was very different from the weather in Connecticut. From the stories that Nanny had told her, the last thing Meg expected to see was a nice hotel, but apparently the remote fisherman's island in the Atlantic where Nanny was raised had become a big tourist attraction. There were now a few hotels and spas that accommodated vacationers on Inishbofin. Meg and her mom ate a wonderful breakfast, with soft, new-age music playing in the background. As they ate, they enjoyed looking out at the incredible scenery that drew the tourists from all over Ireland, and the world, for that matter.

"Meg, we have to go into Cleggan to take care of some business."

"What kind of business?"

"There are no funeral homes on Bofin, and Owen's body was taken there. I have to go to the funeral parlor in Cleggan to make Owen's funeral arrangements." On the walk to the hotel they had decided to call him by his first name instead of the very long title of Great Grandfather O'Flaherty. "Because of your accident, I made the decision that we would take the ferry in."

"The ferry! But, Mom… our vow… I'm not scared. Let's get right back into the *Cailín Mo Chroí*. If we rode a ferry, Nanny would be very disappointed."

"Nanny would be more disappointed to hear that I nearly lost her grandchild to the Atlantic because of our stupid vow."

"Our vow is not stupid. It's the way of our family, and I refuse to take the ferry," Meg said defiantly. "Besides, our family is protected by the fairies. They won't let anything happen to us."

"What are you talking about?"

Meg told her mom about what she had felt when she was being swept out to sea and then explained to her everything Trout had told her about the selkies. Meg had expanded on Trout's theory in her own mind and was convinced that her great grandmother was a selkie that had returned to the sea to keep watch on her family, like their banshee.

"Selkies…You are really losing it, Meg. The hypothermia must have frozen part of your brain. Nanny kept in touch with her mom up until she died."

"Maybe she didn't die? Nanny said that Owen never even told her of her mother's death, and that she had to find out about it from the neighbors. And Trout told me she just disappeared one day. Maybe Owen had discovered her hidden skin and she fled back to sea and he made up the story of her dying to cover it up."

"Perhaps I should have left you at home. I think this has been way too much for a little girl like you to take in."

Meg looked up with pleading eyes, "After all we have been through you still don't believe me?"

"Selkies or not, we are taking the ferry into Cleggan." Meg could tell her mom's mind was set by the stern look she gave. She could also see a trace of fear in her eyes, something she never had seen in her mother. "Either you come with me on the ferry or I will leave you with the Davins. I am not taking the sailboat."

"I made a vow and I don't plan on breaking it," Meg defiantly told her mother.

"Fine," Shay threw up her hands. She looked down at Meg for a long time waiting for her to give in but Meg wouldn't budge. It was their first real argument. Meg stood her ground. She was not going to break her vow and set foot on a motorboat. She knew her mother was scared after what had happened the day before, but Meg was just fine and not scared at all because she knew she was being guarded by the fairies. Shay was not going to back down either, and she didn't say a word to Meg as they walked to the Davins' house. She asked if Meg could stay with them for the day, and they said yes. They then walked Shay back down to the pier, and Meg watched in disbelief as her mom boarded the ferry for Cleggan.

As the ferry cruised out of the harbor Meg saw the *Cailín Mo Chroí* tied up next to a large, luxury motor yacht in the bay that must have been the one owned by Mr. Woods or, The Digger, as Trout called him. The yacht was gorgeous with two levels, tinted windows, and a large afterdeck for swimming—it towered over the small sailboat.

Meg stood on the dock, arms folded, giving her mother the best look of disappointment she could muster until the ferry had disappeared from view. When it was gone Declan walked them down to a beach where his currach was sitting on the sand. Meg asked Declan if it would be okay for Trout to give her a tour of the island. Declan said it was no problem since he needed to go out fishing anyway. Trout liked the idea of being Meg's tour guide around Bofin.

17

The Island of the White Cow

"The first thing you need to know is how the island got its name," Trout began. His father had left to go fishing, and he and Meg were still on the beach. "Thousands of years ago, there was these two fishermen who got stuck in a fog. They rowed about for a couple of hours and found themselves on a misty island that they never knew existed. Now, they had been fishing mackerel all day and were starved, so they lit up a fire on the beach to cook some food."

Meg loved they lyrical way Trout talked. He spoke with a musical cadence and rhythm that complemented his heavy Irish accent.

"As soon as they lit the coals the mist lifted and they saw this woman walking down the beach whippin' on a white cow. Then all of a sudden, the cow turned to stone and the lady disappeared." Trout paused and opened his eyes wide for dramatic effect.

"White cow... Boffin, Bo... Finn? I have a white dog back home in America that my mom named Finn. She said it meant *white* in Irish, so *Bo* must mean *cow*, Island of the White Cow, Inish Bo Finn, Inishbofin." Meg beamed with pride at her ability to piece together some Irish words and figure out their meaning.

"You're a regular Irish speaker, aren't ye," teased Trout.

"Trout, why don't you speak Irish here on Bofin like they do in the Aran Islands?"

"Do ya see those ruins on that island across the harbor?"

Meg looked across and saw the remains of an immense stone fort on top of a rock overlooking the harbor.

"Have ye heard of Cromwell?"

"Yes. My mother told me about that awful man on our way here."

"That's Cromwell's fort. The English were garrisoned there during his war. It was also a prison where they kept all of the Catholic priests they didn't kill on the spot in the rest of Ireland. Priests were outlawed and hunted, you know. It's high tide now but beneath the water in the harbor is a rock called Bishop's Rock. Of all the priests they had imprisoned here, there was only one bishop, so they decided to do something special to him, because he had fought them so. They rowed him out and chained him to the rock at low tide and rowed back to watch from the fort. The tide came in until he was under the water and drowned." Trout looked as angry as if he had been there to watch the atrocity himself. "Cromwell's men stayed here on the island long enough to kill the Irish language from the Bofin Islanders... We had to speak their language or die..." He paused for a second, then looked at her with a sudden twinkle in his eye. "And jaysus, it's a hard language to speak, anyway," he said to lighten the mood. Like the ever-changing weather on the island, Trout could go from gloomy to sunny in an instant.

"Can we go out to the fort?"

"Not now, with the tide up we can't get there on foot. We'll do our side of the island, the West Quarter. And besides, I want to show you some Irish ruins."

Meg and Trout walked up from the beach past many small, brightly painted cottages and green fields with sheep grazing. Inishbofin was about three and a half miles long and almost two miles wide. It was hilly like the shore it faced. The harbor divided the island into two primary areas, the West Quarter where Owen's cottage was, and the North East. Trout told Meg there were two main roads on the island— the high road and the low road—the high located on the hillier western side and the low running through the harbor. These roads were the main arteries of the whole rugged and beautiful island. The wind whipped their jackets as they walked up the low road. While they walked, they talked about their families and school and how they both loved the sea. Meg and Trout had a lot in common, and for the first time in her life, Meg felt as if she could make a friend.

Every now and then they passed an abandoned house with the windows boarded up and walls falling down. Trout told her that the hard life of an islander had chased many families off the island. Inishbofin had as many as a thousand people living here at one time but the number had dwindled down to about two hundred. Trout's family had been on the island since it was founded, as far as he was concerned. And he told her that his father continued to lobster with a traditional currach to please the tourists, even using oars during the tourist season. Fishing for a living had died out on the island only to return with the influx of tourism. His father's "traditional" lobsters were a regular fixture on the posh hotels' menus. Trout told Meg that, for a long time, eating shellfish had been hated by the islanders because it was considered famine food, but that now that sentiment was changing. Just as the hatred of the English had disappeared with the end of the troubles in Ireland, eating shellfish was becoming more acceptable. In the "new" Ireland, long-held notions and objections were melting away.

It was after Bofin's big tourist season, so Meg and Trout were alone on the road except for the sheep and some cows that were allowed to walk anywhere they pleased. The road rose up and they turned back towards the harbor and walked out on top of a flat rock covered in vegetation and a tumbled pile of stones that Trout called *Dun Grania*. Meg looked around at the much less impressive ruins of *Dun Grania* as Trout told her that the sheltered bay had always been an important shipping harbor because of its protection and deep anchorage.

They looked back at the fort. The view from this vantage was much better than it had been from the harbor, and Meg could see why Trout had brought her here. The peninsula the fort was situated on rose up behind the fort to a rocky hill with scattered patches of green grass. The fort walls rose up from a rock that protruded into the harbor.

"Before Cromwell, the fort over there was the castle of a Spanish pirate called Don Bosco. Bosco had allied himself with Granuaile, for whom the ruins on this side of the harbor were named."

"Who's Granuaile?" asked Meg

"Who's Granuaile?" Trout was stunned. "She was the Sea Queen of Ireland, Grania Ni Mhaille, Grace O'Malley, the greatest Irish sea captain of her time. She controlled all the waters of Connemara from her castle on Clare Island just north of here. You haven't heard of her?"

"No." But Meg wanted to know more. "A woman pirate?"

"Of course." Trout then thought twice about his answer. "Well, it depends on who's talkin' about her. To the Irish, she was a great female chieftain of the O'Malley clan with a fleet of ships patrolling her seas. But to the English, she was a murderous pirate. It's all about perspective, ya know."

"Of course," said Meg, egging him on.

"She and Don Bosco ran a chain from here to the fort," he pointed across the water, "and would trap ships that came into the harbor. They would charge them a fee for safe passage. Granuaile knew these waters like the back of her hand and the foreign ships had to pay or be sunk."

"Sounds like good business. She was a regular tour guide."

"Smart woman she was... Don Bosco and her made a killin' for a while but they had a fallin' out of sorts and Granuaile ended up chasin' him off the island. Before he was chased off, he supposedly buried a treasure under his castle. They say he had put a Spanish curse on it so that only he could dig it up.

"Long ago, there was a priest on the island who tried to find the treasure. He snuck out to the castle one night and started to look, but as he was digging, he heard a voice speaking in Irish from below the ground that told him to stop. Thinking he heard a voice from hell, he ran away and never returned to the castle."

Meg looked across the harbor at the ruins. She felt differently about the fort now from when she heard about it the first time. She went from feeling utter disgust toward an oppressive English-ruled fortress to an overwhelming urge to explore an abandoned pirate castle.

"Trout, you gotta get me out to that castle."

"I guess we could see if me da is back from fishing. It's startin' to get a bit foggy and he might've come in."

Meg looked around her and was astonished to see that a light fog had indeed started to roll in off the water. The weather on Bofin was as mysterious as the island itself. She and Trout turned their backs to Dun Grania and made their way back down the low road to the harbor.

18

The Corsairs Castle

By the time the time Meg and Trout reached the harbor, the fog had fully set in and they found Declan Davin on the shore unloading the currach with his other son, Dennis. They had just started down into the water to lift the currach up on the beach when they saw Trout and Meg approaching.

"How's Trout?" Declan called out.

"Fine, Da. Megeen wants to go and see the fort and the tide's only just goin' out."

"Well, why don't ya wait till the tide's out?"

"You know how these Yanks are. Everything has to be right now, and Megeen, after beatin' the ocean before, tinks nothing can stop her, not even a fog."

"So what are ye askin'?"

"We just want to row the currach over, and seein' as you're not in need of it, I don't want to disappoint the great granddaughter of The O'Flaherty."

"Oh ya don't, do ya? All right, Trout," Declan said, handing him a line. "And you, Miss Megeen, stay out of the water or I'll have both of your hides, O'Flaherty or no."

Trout, in his big rubber boots, walked out in the water and held the boat as Declan lifted Meg into the currach. There was a pair of oars still in their locks and Meg grabbed the ones in the bow while Trout sat aft. She looked down at the oars, noticing they didn't have a wide paddle blade at the end as Meg was used to. Rather, they were just skinny and thin, for skimming on the top of the water, Trout said. The currach was incredibly light and sat on the water like no boat she had ever been on. The slightest pull of the oar moved it incrementally more than Meg thought it would. Had Trout not been with her, she would have twirled around in circles, but with a little coaching they were soon gliding through the quiet, fog-locked harbor. Although they couldn't see much through the fog, they could hear the waves on the shore and the clanking of lines and tackle hitting boats somewhere in the mist. They passed the *Cailín Mo Chroí* that was still tied up to Mr. Woods's boat and noticed that the huge yacht had a light on in the cabin.

They rowed a ways farther, and through the fog they could see the ruins of the castle looming on top of its rocky home. Beyond that, they barely saw a lighthouse that guarded the harbor entrance. Since the tide was going out, the ghostly specter of Bishop's Rock rose out of the water like an evil presence pointing to the clouds. Trout pointed it out to her, and just the sight of it made the hair on Meg's arms stand on end. They rowed past the rock and soon pulled into a small cove with a beach. Trout jumped out and helped Meg get on shore. They pulled the currach up in the beach as high as they could, then tied a rope to a large rock above the waterline.

"What was that back there, Trout? All the Yank stuff. And my name is *Margaret*, not *Megeen*," Meg said indignantly.

"I got us the boat, didn't I? And us callin' ya Megeen is something nice. It's like callin' ya *Little Meg*."

"I thought that was *Meg Beag* in Irish."

"Maybe out on the Aran Islands. Not here," Trout said with a smile.

"I guess you're right. Sorry."

"Not to worry. Just stay close and watch where ya step."

They walked up a well-worn path over a rocky hill passing a few grazing sheep who barely acknowledged their presence. From the top of the hill the fog had temporarily obstructed what was probably an amazing view. Fog has a certain magic of its own—Meg could hear the waves lapping the shore and sea birds cawing from some hidden place but was not able to see any more than the contrast of the green down below and the silvery-grey mist that surrounded them. Trout led her down the hill and they were soon able to make out the ruins that lay below. The stone fortress rose out of the mist the closer they got to it.

It was much bigger than it seemed from afar. The stones of the fort perched precariously on the rock at the mouth of the harbor appeared as if they could be easily pushed into the water. Towering over them, the walls rose up from the green grass in a jumbled mass of stone and cement. They entered the grey walls through the Spanish arch, as Trout called it, which was a large, carved stone that was perched on other larger rocks that held up a wall of stone and mortar. The fog that enveloped them added to the mystery of the ancient ruins that surrounded them.

"Before the Spaniards built this castle there was a fort here. The rock below us is a perfect spot to defend the harbor entrance."

They walked through the structures that were enclosed within the fort. Wall after wall of roofless buildings blended themselves into the grey sky. Meg found the smell of the sea and the moss-covered rocks amid the grass intoxicating. She had never set foot in something so old and her imagination was reeling. There were openings in the walls both high and low that must have been used for defending the castle. Meg and Trout looked out a small window opening to the fog-shrouded bay. In her mind, Meg was able to envision a chain strung over the water and a boat trapped in the harbor.

How incredible it must be, Meg thought, to live among such amazing ruins. But Trout didn't seem to be the least bit impressed. Meg supposed that when you live next to something like this castle it eventually becomes just a pile of rocks you take tourists out to. Sunlight streaming through the fog gave the entire place an eerie look. The mist was like a silk veil that, if pulled back, would reveal a thriving pirate castle from the past. Trout and Meg walked between more stone walls and made their way into a courtyard that was situated in the center of the castle.

"So where did the priest dig for the treasure?" Meg asked.

Before Trout could respond, a man's voice pierced the mist. "That's just an old folktale," he said, startling them. The voice came from the direction of the Spanish arch where they had first walked in. Trout and Meg jumped at the sound but, Meg recognized the strange accent. Al Woods stepped into the courtyard.

"The Digger," Trout whispered.

"His name is Mr. Woods, Trout."

"You can call me Al."

"Just Al?" asked Trout.

"Alonzo if you wish."

"Alonzo…Wasn't that Don Bosco's name?"

"You're correct, young man. *Don* is an honorific used in Spain, just like *Sir* is used in English. It's usually reserved for royalty, but in this case it was a self-proclaimed title of the Barbary corsair, Alonzo Bosco."

"Al…onzo, what are you doing here?"

"I saw you two rowing out here and thought I should make sure you were safe. It's not a good idea for two little kids to be walking around old ruins in the fog."

"Thanks, Mr. Woods. I just wanted to see the old fort," Meg said.

"Did you come to see an old fort or a corsair's castle? I thought I heard you ask where the pirate treasure was."

"You know about the treasure?" Trout and Meg said in unison.

"I know quite a bit about pirates and I'm kind of an expert on Don Bosco, you could say. Actually, his treasure is long gone."

"Cromwell," theorized Trout.

"On the contrary, Don Bosco's treasure was gone long before Oliver Cromwell arrived on Inishbofin. In fact, it was moved to a new location shortly after Don Bosco was chased off the island."

The more Meg heard Al talk, the less she could figure out where his accent was from. It was not American or British, yet his English was very proper.

"I've never heard any of this, and I should know. My family has been here forever," challenged Trout.

"No one knows about the true story of Don Bosco, except me," Al countered. He gave them a strange look of one who knows a secret. "After a long and prosperous partnership, he was double-crossed by the sea witch who drove him from Inishbofin and stole his treasure. I have been coming here for years searching for the key to find where she hid it."

"The key, a sea witch… Who are you talking about?" asked Meg.

"I'm talking about the conniving, treacherous, pirate witch Grace O'Malley," Alonzo said, pronouncing the name as if he was spitting out poison.

"She wasn't a witch. She was a queen," said Trout.

"She was a witch who enchanted Don Bosco, then double-crossed him and stole his half of their treasure," Alonzo said, drawing nearer to the kids, his dark eyes wide. He regained his composure and said, "They had plundered a lot of gold together, nearly two million pounds. Don Bosco kept his half safe in a secret chamber below this castle, and it was guarded by a Jinn, or Genie."

"A genie, like in Aladdin? I thought they were in Arabia in magic lamps. You're trying to spook us!"

"Don Bosco was a Muslim Moor and the Jinn existed in their beliefs. They could be assigned the task of guarding an object."

"Like a treasure!"

"Exactly," Alonzo continued. "Granuaile surprised him one night with a fleet of ships and chased him from Inishbofin threatening to kill him if he ever returned to these waters. A few months afterwards, Don Bosco disguised himself as a fisherman, snuck back on the island and, much to his dismay, found that she had defeated his Jinn and stolen his plunder. She had even summoned an Irish spirit to guard the empty chamber."

"What a story," said Meg.

"Brilliant," said Trout, "it all makes sense now, the old story of the priest searching for the treasure told that the voice he heard from below the ground spoke to him in Irish to stop digging. That part never made sense to me, seein' it was a Spanish curse."

"Indeed, Grace O'Malley was a *bruja*, a witch. It was her curse that guarded the secret chamber after Don Bosco left."

Meg didn't bother to fight with Alonzo about Granuaile, and although Trout seemed bugged, he held his tongue also. Alonzo was an archeologist and Meg decided that he could probably help them learn more about the treasure. She asked him if he could give them a tour of the fort and tell them all about it.

Alonzo walked them around the ruins explaining to them how Cromwell had turned the castle into a seventeenth-century, star-shaped fort using much of the existing castle left by Don Bosco. Originally built as a barracks for Cromwell's army, the fort was later used to hold the clergy that they had captured. From here, the priests were sent out around the British Empire to be sold as slaves. The English held the fort for a long time and used it later on to curtail the activities of French pirates who used the harbors on the west coast of Ireland to hide out.

Alonzo showed them a well in the center courtyard, explaining that it held a hidden entrance to the secret chamber. He also said that he had located the chamber himself, but that he would not show Meg and Trout where it was. He quickly followed that up to say that when he entered the treasure room the spirit that guarded it must have left and there was no clue as to where the treasure had been moved. Alonzo was very informative yet guarded at the same time, and Meg sensed he was not telling them all he knew.

After the guided tour they walked from the fort back over the hill and to the foggy cove. Alonzo helped them into the currach and guided them back in his skiff to the other side of the harbor.

While they glided through the water Meg tried to make sense of everything she had heard. Granuaile and Don Bosco were partners and had plundered two million pounds of gold, and Grania later moved it. That was the first part that didn't make sense to her. How in the world could anyone carry or move a million pounds of gold? That is so heavy! Also, if Granuaile beat the genie and cleared out the treasure chamber, why would she put an Irish spirit there to guard it? It was just not adding up.

"Trout, I have been thinking about all of this treasure stuff and I can't figure out a couple of things. First of all, how could anybody carry around a million pounds of gold?"

Trout said "Why? How much do you think it weighed?"

"A million pounds."

"Yeah. What do you think?"

"I don't know. That's why I'm asking you."

Trout looked at her and laughed so hard he nearly fell out of the boat. His laughter echoed around the harbor and Meg furrowed her brow, questioning why he was laughing.

"A million pounds…That's brilliant. You tink it's a weight!" He said in between laughs, "I tink he was talking about its value not the weight. Pounds was what our money was called before the Euro."

Meg blushed and then laughed at herself, too. Soon they were left on the beach on the other side of the harbor, where they said goodbye to Al. Meg never got to ask Trout about the spirit.

19

Bald Grace

Meg's head was racing from all she had experienced over the past two days. She had gone from her normal world of family, school, and play to one filled with banshees, selkies, genies, pirates, and treasure. Her old existence back in Connecticut was dreary in comparison to the life and history of Ireland. Although Meg didn't know much about Grace O'Malley, she wanted to learn everything she could about her. She wondered if there was a way to figure out why she put a spirit to guard an empty chamber. Trout and Meg left the harbor and walked back to the West Quarter where Owen's cottage and the Davin's house were located.

When they got back to Trout's house, his mother Nell told them that the return ferry from Cleggan had been canceled due to the fog and that Meg was to stay with the Davins for the night until her mom could return. The news didn't bother Meg; she was still mad at her mom and she was kind of relieved to not have to go back to Owen's dreary cottage. Besides, she wanted to learn more about Grace O'Malley, and she knew Trout was the one to tell her.

Trout and Meg headed back outside and climbed up on the stone wall that was in front of Trout's house. They sat there a moment in silence before Meg resumed her questioning. "Trout, why is Grace O'Malley known by so many different names?"

"First of all, stop calling her Grace O'Malley. That's the English version of her name. She's called Granuaile. Her given name was Grania and she was the daughter of the chieftain of the *O'Maille* clan, the greatest sea-faring family that Ireland had ever seen. Her father was *Eoghan Dubhdara O'Maille*, Owen "Black Oak" O'Malley, who ruled the land and sea just north of Bofin around Clew Bay. Grania was Owen's only child with his wife Maeve. Owen also had a son *Donal-na-Pioppa*, Donal of the Pipes, who was illegitimate, but Owen treated him as his son regardless.

"Grania got the name Granuaile because, even though she was the best sailor in the O'Malley fleet, her father refused to take her on a trading trip to Spain because he said her long hair would get caught in the ships ropes. Furious and not to be stopped, Grania cut off all of her long, red hair, which took away Owen's excuse and forced him to take her on the voyage. From then on they called her *Grania Mhaol*, Grania the Bald, which was shortened to *Granuaile*. And after that, the name stuck."

"So Granuaile became a sea captain?" Meg asked.

"Indeed she did—the greatest and most fierce captain in Ireland."

Meg was suddenly struck by the similarity between the story of Granuaile and that of her Nanny. They both forced an unwilling father to take them out to sea. Her thoughts jumped to the compendium, which was inscribed with the letter *G*! Meg grabbed Trout by the arm and dragged him to Owen's cottage, where she pulled out the special birthday gift she had received from her grandmother. She held it up for Trout to see.

"Would ya look at that... What is it?"

"My grandmother gave it to me. It's been handed down in our family from generation to generation. It's an astronomical compendium."

"An astro what?"

"It's a tool used by sea captains to navigate the oceans. Look here, Trout, there's a *G* on the front," Meg said. With eyes aglow, she pointed to the Gaelic script *G* engraved in the brass.

"Oh, Megeen, you're gonna love this next part. In order to expand their territory, Granuaile was married to *Dónal Ó Flaithbheartaigh*, Donal O'Flaherty. He was heir to the O'Flaherty clan who ruled *Iar Connacht*, all of the land of western Connemara including Inishbofin. You must be a descendant of Granuaile!"

A sudden flash of knowing flowed through Meg's mind and she thought she felt a tingle coming from the compendium. She looked at it and then at Trout, full of pride at her newfound ancestry. At that moment she felt as if she had grown an inch taller. She held her chin high and looked out on the world with different eyes. Meg was true royalty, a descendant of the Sea Queen of Ireland. She realized her mother must have known all this because she had given her the middle name Grace!

"I'm a pirate princess!" she yelled, her voice lifting to the rafters of her great grandfather's cottage. Trout gave her a corrective glance by raising one eyebrow. Meg thought better of what she had said. "*Irish* princess?"

At that, they both laughed. Meg was fascinated to learn the details of Grace O'Malley's exploits, and so Trout recounted all he knew.

Young Grace's early life was spent both on the Atlantic Ocean in ships and in the many castles and forts that had belonged to her family on the coast and some of the islands around Clew Bay. The O'Malleys taxed all of the fishermen who came to their coast, and they were very powerful and one of the few great seafaring families in Ireland. Grania's knowledge of the sea became legendary and her skill was unmatched. Her parents made sure Grania was well educated. As a result of her fine education and many distant travels, Grania was very worldly and spoke several different languages.

The O'Malley clan had the gift of predicting the weather by the look of the ocean. Grania's father Owen had taken Donal-na-Pioppa out on his galley one day to see if he had inherited the O'Malley gift, and a young Grania had come along for the ride. Looking out on the Atlantic, Donal saw nothing. But Grania looked out too, and told her father that a storm was brewing. Sure enough, one hit. When it did, Owen knew Grania was the next great O'Malley.

Eventually the time came for to be married. Her parents had found a good political match for her in Donal O'Flaherty. In ancient Ireland, marriages were more about connections and power and less about love. Granuaile had three children with Donal: Owen, Maeve, and Murrough, but she never settled down to the life of a housewife. Her nautical talent and fiery spirit eclipsed that of her husband, and before long, she was the captain of the O'Flaherty fleet.

She led her family's army and navy in many skirmishes and battles with neighboring clans, and her reputation was like that of no woman of her time. She was fearless and courageous and never sat out a fight. Her exploits in Connacht led to a ban on O'Flaherty ships in Galway harbor, reminding Meg of the old sign in that city her mother told her about, "from the ferocious O'Flahertys, may God protect us."

Undeterred from the Galway ban and wanting to expand her power and reach, Grace decided to take her business elsewhere. She made trading voyages to Spain, Portugal, Scotland, and Ulster. On these trips Granuaile had a habit of capturing any slow-moving merchant ships she happened to come across. She continued to tax the fishermen that fished her family's waters and so her power grew.

Granuaile's husband Donal was prone to argument and was constantly getting into trouble himself. On one occasion he battled with a rival clan, the Joyces, and took from them one of their castles on Lough Corrib, a large lake in Galway. When the Joyces tried to take it back, Donal fought them so hard that they nicknamed him *An Cullagh*, "The Cock." Donal held the fort for a while, but eventually the Joyces defeated him, killing him in battle. In honor of how ferociously he had fought, when the Joyces reclaimed their castle, they renamed it Cock's Castle.

Granuaile's grief and fury over her husband's death led her to return to Cock's Castle and take it back with an army of O'Flahertys. The battle was fierce and bloody, but Granuaile came away victorious. From then on the castle was called *Caislean an Cearca,* "Hens Castle," and Granuaile held it for the rest of her days.

"Women did not inherit their husband's land or title in those days, so with no husband, Grania was forced to move back to the O'Malley's castle on Clare Island and back into the fold of her own clan. She was so beloved by the O'Flahertys that many took their ships and followed her to the O'Malley stronghold, remaining loyal to Granuaile herself. Her fleet was vast, indeed.

The O'Malleys now controlled most of Clew Bay and Connemara except for a small section near Newport and Rockfleet Castle that was held by Iron Richard Bourke, an Anglo-Norman aristocrat who was in line to be elected *The Mac William,* the second most powerful position in all of Connacht. So, to expand her lands and power, Grania married him. Their marriage was that of equals, and with Richard, she bore a son, Theobald. His nickname, "Tibbot of the Ships," came because Granuaile gave birth to him on a ship.

The story goes that, just after childbirth, Grania's ship came under attack by corsairs, and her men were having trouble winning without her. The captain went below to where she was nursing her newborn son and begged her to come up on deck and rally her men. Still exhausted from childbirth, Granuaile was furious that her men were powerless without her and had the audacity to ask for her help. When she went up she cried to them, "May you be seven times worse off this day next year for not being able to do without me for one day." She stormed out in her robe with sword and pistol in hand and led her men to victory.

Every story Meg heard made her fall more in love with her unbelievable ancestor. The more she heard, the more she was mad that she had never known of Granuaile until now. How could her mother not have told her these stories? They were more amazing and fantastic then any fairy tale she had ever heard. Granuaile's name should be as well-known throughout the world as the names of the English Queens.

"Granuile." Meg pronounced the name as if under her magical spell. "I wish I had known about her before."

"Maybe yer ma never knew either?" Trout replied.

"That's impossible. She knows all about Ireland and all of the legends. She has to know about Granuaile."

"What if she knew the legend but never made the connection?"

"Oh, Trout," said Meg with a smile. "That has to be it! She knew nothing about her family until just recently. I can't wait to tell her."

At that moment, Trout's mom called out from the house for them to come in for dinner.

20

A Talk Queen to Queen

The Davin's house, although close in proximity to Meg's great grandfather's house, was light-years away in comfort. They had a cozy living room with a TV and a glass enclosed fireplace that was much like the one her family had at home. The house had three bedrooms: one for the parents, one for the boys Dennis and Trout, and one for the youngest Davin, Deirdre. Trout's little sister was four years old and cute as a button, and Meg soon learned that American girls were not the only ones who came under the Disney princess spell.

Nell Davin told Meg that she would be sleeping in Deirdre's room. When she showed it to her, it was as if Meg were stepping back in time to her own room of just a year or two earlier. The walls were covered with the same smiling faces of the princesses Meg had worshipped as a little girl. The colors pink and purple dominated the room and dolls and accessories occupied nearly every square inch. Meg was surprised to learn that little Deirdre's favorite was Belle from *Beauty and the Beast*, rather than Ariel, *The Little Mermaid*, who was Meg's favorite. But then, every little girl had her own reasons for loving her favorite princess.

Meg played with Deirdre in her room while waiting for dinner. She loved how Deirdre talked. The more time Meg spent in Ireland the easier it was for her to understand the

Irish people she talked to. Irish accents have a speed that Meg had a hard time catching up to at first. But Meg was learning that the different tones and inflections often indicated as much meaning to the listener as the words themselves. Earlier that day, when Meg was talking to Trout, she started to feel as though her way of talking was slow. At one point, Meg asked Trout to speak with an American accent, which he did. But he came across as sounding like California surfer dude, which Meg found hilarious.

Deirdre's Irish accent made playing princess a totally new experience for Meg. When Meg pronounced Beauty's name, *Belle*, it sounded just like the word *bell*. When Deirdre said the word *Belle*, however, it wasn't a plain, flat pronunciation. It gained an extra vowel sound, like *baell*, and also dipped and rose in tone. Many of the words spoken by Meg's new Irish friends were the same she used, but they had a musical tone she had never heard before. And, although her grandmother spoke with an Irish accent, over the years it had lost much of the unique character it must have had when she first arrived in America.

When the Davin family sat down for dinner, Meg had picked up enough of the Irish accent that she didn't miss a word that was said. Declan told them all about his shortened fishing day and kidded Meg about her skills rowing a currach. Trout's brother Dennis asked her many questions about America. Unfortunately, television shows were their only glimpse of American culture, and Dennis had a lot of misconceptions about American life which Meg tried to explain away as much as she could, given her young age.

Trout and Meg told the family about their adventure at the Fort and her newly discovered link to Granuaile. Trout's mother was particularly interested in the connection as she was apparently a big fan of Granuaile. While they ate, Nell told them more tales of Granuaile. The most amazing story of all was about the time Grania sailed to London, England. There she went up the Thames River to the royal palace, where she requested a personal meeting with England's Queen Elizabeth.

At the time of Grania, Connacht for the most part was still Irish, although some of the larger towns and cities such as Galway were controlled by the English. Often, this control was held by Anglo-Normans who had assimilated into their surroundings and had some Irish leanings. The so-called Tribes of Galway were a group of these Anglo-Normans, and had been having a long-time problem with Granuaile. Much of their animosity towards her was because, as a harbor city, the Galway tribes imposed tariffs and taxes on the ships and traders within their walls and, when those same people left the harbor, Granuaile taxed them again for going through her waters. This led to many fights between the tribes and the O'Flahertys and Grania, and eventually resulted in the sign that was erected at the gates of the city.

Grania was a very smart woman. She knew which way the political tide was moving, and offered her army to the English early on to help them in any way they wanted. Granuaile didn't act out of love for the English but rather used her cunning and guile to always remain a step ahead of her enemies. Because of this she gained favor with the Lord Deputy of Ireland, and when the tribes went to Dublin to formally accuse her of piracy because of the taxes she collected, their accusation was largely ignored.

Granuaile's ships patrolled the waters around much of Ireland, raiding castles and ships and then disappearing into the many hidden coves and bays on the Irish coast. She controlled and exercised her power from the many castles and fortresses in the northwest part of Ireland where she was out of the reach of any English influence. The O'Malleys and Grania had things under control until a new foe entered the picture.

A newly appointed Governor of Connacht, Richard Bingham, attempted to gain more control over the local lords. One way he tried to do this was by offering English titles and lands to the Irish chieftains in his territory. Many accepted those offers, but never the O'Malleys or the O'Flahertys, and this infuriated Bingham. As Granuaile's power and influence grew, Bingham made many attempts at removing her but he was never successful. He declared her the biggest threat in Connacht to the English, and in his reports to the crown had even called her "nurse to all rebellions" all over Ireland. The governor soon declared war on her family. In 1593 Richard Bingham tricked and killed Granuaile's oldest son Owen and imprisoned her other sons, Tibbot and Murrough, along with her half-brother Donal-na-Pioppa.

Grania was sixty-three years old at the time and, although still feisty, she was getting tired of the constant battling and came up with an idea to save herself and her family. She decided that the only way to stop Bingham was to go over his head to his boss, Queen Elizabeth of England. She set sail for London to demand a meeting queen to queen.

Upon her arrival in London, Granuaile's connection to the Lord Deputy of Ireland came in handy again, and he was able to help her arrange the meeting. Grania was sent of series of questions from the queen, which she thoughtfully answered and returned. The queen must have liked what she read because a meeting was scheduled shortly after, at Elizabeth's palace in Greenwich.

At the appointed time, the accused pirate queen entered the court of Queen Elizabeth dressed in a fine gown. In spite of her age and fine clothes, she was escorted into the queen's chamber under heavy guard due to her reputation. The room, filled with courtiers and guards, fell into silence as Granuaile approached with her head held high. The lords and ladies waited with baited breath in anticipation of the first words of the notorious woman. Grania broke the silence with a sneeze and one of the noblemen extended a delicate silk handkerchief, which she accepted. Grania blew her nose loudly into the cloth and then threw it into the fire. Everyone gasped with indignation. Grania looked around at all the fancy people and told them that, in her country, they did not keep such soiled things, underhandedly insulting those present. She further amazed the crowd by walking up to address the queen without first bowing. Grania intentionally did not bow because she did not recognize Elizabeth as a superior, but rather as an equal.

Queen Elizabeth was extremely interested in this woman before her, and none of Grania's egregious behavior prevented the meeting from proceeding. The queen welcomed her, and the two powerful women, who were nearly the same age, sat down for a chat. No one knows what was said between them, but Elizabeth must have taken to the sea queen, because Granuaile emerged from the meeting with a letter that directed Bingham to free her family and to leave her and her kin alone for the rest of her days.

"I have read about Queen Elizabeth in my history books and even saw a movie about her. Why haven't I ever heard about Granuaile?" Meg asked aloud.

Trout's father said, "'cause history is written by the victors, not the vanquished."

Trout spoke up, "Granuaile is famous in Ireland. She has been written about in story and in song since her time, and is even in the old rebel song 'Óró, Sé do Bheatha 'Bhaile.' Do you know it?"

Meg shook her head no and Trout sang:

"Tá Gráinne Mhaol ag teacht thar sáile,
Óglaigh armtha léi mar gharda,
Gaeil iad féin is ní Gaill ná Spáinnigh,
Is cuirfidh siad ruaig ar Ghallaibh."

Trout had a nice singing voice. When he finished, Meg teased, "I thought you couldn't speak Irish."

"I can't, but I do know a couple of songs. It means: Grania the Bald is coming over the sea, armed warriors along with her as her guard, they are Irishmen, not French nor Spanish... And they will rout the foreigners!"

Trout's parents beamed with pride at their son's knowledge. As they finished their meal Meg was bubbling over with excitement from all the information she had just heard. "I can't believe I'm related to such a famous woman!"

"You'd better be careful who you tell this to, Meg, especially our friend Alonzo. He seems to have a hate for your relative."

"What do you mean?"

"All of that sea witch stuff he said. I swear that, every time he spoke her name today, he wanted to spit on the ground."

"I wonder why," Meg asked aloud.

They spent the rest of the night talking of castles and battles and the plight of the Irish. Trout's family was very well educated and proud of their heritage and taught Meg a lot. She thought it was one of the best days of her life. When it was time to go to sleep, Meg headed to Deirdre's room and got into bed with the compendium still hanging around her neck. She had decided she wanted to keep it on all of the time now, no matter how big or heavy it was.

21

A Sad Day

There must be something about the air on an Irish island because that night Meg had the most vivid dream of her life. She was standing on the deck of a Galway hooker. Its crimson sails billowed overhead. She took out the compendium and held it up to take a course reading. In the sun, it shined like a golden mirror as she dialed coordinates into the volvelle. The deck was heaving up and down in heavy Atlantic swells, and Meg yelled out orders to her crew, who readily obeyed. She looked out to starboard and saw a corsair ship rapidly approaching, and called out to her crew to be on the ready for battle. The dark-skinned captain of the corsair was standing on the bow of his ship, calling for her to hand over her treasure. She yelled back defiantly "Never!" and turned the tiller hard to the right to ram her foe. Then she woke up.

The Davins were sitting at the table eating breakfast when Meg walked in. Her head still awash in her dream, Meg did not notice that they were all nicely dressed. They told her that the fog had lifted at some time during the night and Shay was on her way back to Inishbofin. After breakfast they walked down to the harbor to meet the ferry and her.

The argument that had separated them and Meg's anger toward her mother for taking a ferry had all but washed away.

In fact, she was so excited she could not wait to see her mom step foot on the pier so she could run up, hug her, and tell her all about her discovery. Her plan for the day was to walk out to the castle with her mom and see if they could find some clues as to where the treasure might be or the entrance to the secret chamber.

The sky was grey and the water dark and choppy. Meg kept glancing at the castle the whole walk over, unable to take her eyes off it as they waited on the pier. They were going to find the treasure, she knew it. The ferry came around the lighthouse next to the fort and slowly entered the harbor. There were a lot of people standing at the pier and Meg wondered why. Trout said nothing, but his mother and father greeted most of the people there with a solemn hello. Then she saw it. On the deck of the ferry, her mother was standing next to a wooden casket with a flag of dark red and white draped over it. Trout told her the flag was the colors of Galway and that nothing would be open on the island that day. Owen was coming home to be buried, and his people were there to greet him.

Six men, including Declan, walked to the end of the dock and hoisted the casket above their shoulders. They carried it down the pier, past the onlookers, and towards the church. The islanders joined the slow procession. Shay was following the casket, and when they went past the waiting Davins, she reached out for Meg and they walked together in silence. People standing on the road bowed their heads when the procession walked by. Meg looked up to her mom and saw she had tears in her eyes. Meg started crying too.

St. Colman's church was not far from the pier. As they approached the church, Meg saw more people standing outside waiting. At the back of the crowd, wearing his fedora hat, she noticed Alonzo Woods. He held up his hand in greeting, but she didn't wave back.

They were ushered into the chapel. It was painted in bright red, blue, and yellow. The stained glass windows shed what little light they could, given the overcast day. Church was something the Murphys rarely attended back home, except on special religious holidays and for an occasional baptism, mostly because Shay and Mark always had work to do on Sundays.

The smoke of incense hung in the air as the priest said the funeral mass. Towards the end, the priest recounted the first time he met The O'Flaherty.

Owen was walking the shore as was his custom, and the priest asked why he did what he did. "I'm waitin' and watchin," was his reply. "For what?" asked the priest. "For my Kathleen to come home."

The mention of Owen waiting for Nanny to return to him sent Meg and Shay into hysterics. They held onto one another crying convulsively and they heard more wailing from the people gathered behind them.

He was looking for Nanny, not her brother, Meg thought. *I don't ever want to get so mad at my mom that I never talk to her or see her again.*

After the service the pall bearers carried the casket back down to the pier where the *Cailín Mo Chroí* was now tied up. Meg was not sure what was going on, and asked, "Mommy, what's happening?"

"We're taking him to his home where he grew up. That's where he wanted to be buried."

The men carefully loaded the casket on the boat and tied it down. Declan, Trout, the priest, and a few other men stayed on the boat and helped Meg and Shay on board. Just before they cast off from the pier, Meg could not believe her eyes. They hoisted white sails on the Galway hooker. Someone must have changed the sails at some point over night because when Meg rowed past it the day before, it still had red sails.

"He was a king" Meg whispered to Trout.

"He was The O'Flaherty, the last man of his clan."

They sailed out of the harbor and turned right following the shore towards the island that was just south of Inishbofin. Trout told Meg it was called Inishark, or Shark, for short. It was a deserted island whose last inhabitants were evacuated by the Irish Government in 1960. The Shark islanders were forced to leave their home because there was no good harbor on the island, and they would sometimes go months without aid from the mainland when the weather was stormy. Many of the younger islanders had emigrated and the aging population was too much of a liability for the government. The Shark islanders were all given land on the coast, and it has been uninhabited ever since.

When the boat neared the island they dropped the sails and rowed the last hundred yards to a tiny, shallow cove with a small, rocky ramp at the end protected by a dilapidated sea wall. Meg could see that in any kind of bad weather it would be impossible to land here, and she wondered how hard it must have been to live on Shark.

Shark was a big hill of an island beaten by the wind and waves of the Atlantic Ocean. Due to the absence of a good harbor, the Shark islanders had led an isolated existence compared to their close neighbor to the north. At the head of the cove where they had come in, Meg saw a rusted old hand winch on the hill. It must have once been used to pull the boats up on shore. The men on board tied the hooker to the old pier. They then hoisted the casket on their shoulders and marched slowly through deserted fields where only sheep roamed. As they walked, Trout told Meg that Bofin islanders still used Shark for grazing their animals. They walked past roofless cottages, long ago abandoned, until they reached the ruins of a church that was surrounded by weather-beaten gravestones.

The church, they were told, was called St. Leos. It had been built on the site of a seventh-century monastery that was founded by a monk named Leo. It had been a very small church from what was left of it. The priest told them that, in the church's heyday, the Shark Island women would carry their own stools to church on Sundays, as there were no pews in St. Leos. The men used to stand along the outside walls during the service.

The pall bearers lowered the casket into a freshly dug grave that overlooked the ocean. The priest splashed holy water over it as they said a final prayer for Owen O'Flaherty, the last in his family line. Everyone present helped throw the dirt back onto the grave. Meg looked out to the Atlantic Ocean so loved by her family—it seemed even wilder here. Inishark had quite a different feel from Bofin. It occurred to Meg that they were standing on the edge, on the very last bit of Ireland before it met the vast, wide ocean. The mood was somber and the wind whipped everyone as they worked to cover the grave. After the last shovelful was thrown, Meg felt the mood change and the men began to smile.

"A long life is to be celebrated, not mourned," Declan declared as they walked back to the boat. When they reached the pier, one of the men told Meg and Shay that they had to take the white sails down and put the red sails back up. Knowing this would take some time, Meg and her mom wandered off to take a look inside one of the cottages that still had a roof.

The front door was hanging loosely on a rusted hinge. Shay carefully pushed the door open to reveal a cottage identical to Owen's back on Bofin. A chair was pulled up to an empty fireplace and dusty cabinets lined the walls. A solitary plate rested on the table in the same spot where it had been left many years ago.

"Most took all they could when they left, but some left it all," Trout said. He had entered the cottage behind them. "They didn't want anything that reminded them of home when they was evacuated."

The three said nothing as they wandered around the deserted island, listening only to the sound of the wind. The image of the abandoned cabin stayed with Meg as they traveled back to Bofin under the red sails.

22

A Strange Offer

It seemed that all of the people who lived on Bofin Island came out to celebrate the life of Owen O'Flaherty. The pub was packed. Men and women were seated in groups, talking about the news of the day, and kids were running around everywhere, excited at the big gathering. In a corner of the pub a group of musicians was playing lively music. Everyone swayed and tapped their feet to the rhythm.

Shay and Meg sat at a table with the Davins, who entertained them with more stories of Inishbofin. Declan told them that Owen really didn't speak to many people on Bofin, but he had managed to get a story from him now and then.

Long ago, Owen's family had fled to Shark to hide from the English. It was the perfect place because of the difficulty landing on its shores. Owen traveled the world captaining ships, and on one particularly stormy day he was forced to stay on Bofin until conditions permitted him to land back at his home on Shark. He was walking along the beach in the West Quarter, looking out at the unreachable Shark Island, when he happened upon his future wife. He fell madly in love. Owen was so in love, he moved to Inishbofin to be with her and they soon married. With raised eyebrow, Meg shot Trout a glance at the mention of her great grandmother.

A little old man in a tweed hat got up from his chair. A hush fell on those gathered as they knew what was coming. The man sang a sad song of a young immigrant who had left Ireland for America. Each song verse told the story of letters sent back and forth between the young man and the family he had left behind. And each verse ended with the man promising he will soon return home to visit, but he never does. Everyone in the pub nodded their heads in understanding, as no family on Bofin had been spared the sorrow of losing a family member to the dream of a better life through immigration.

After the song ended, the din of the crowd grew louder and the rhythm of the music picked up. A few people got up to dance. Declan raised his glass and made a toast to the memory of Owen O'Flaherty. The table replied with the traditional Irish *Slainte*, meaning *health* or *to your health*. More and more people joined in to dance. Even Trout dragged Meg out to the dance floor to teach her a few *céilí* dances.

The céilí was Ireland's traditional folk dance. It was very similar to square dancing. Pairs of dancers stood in rows facing other couples, each dancing back and forth in a one-two-three jig. Meg had never had so much fun. Like waves crashing on the shore, the lines of people first moved in toward each other and then back out. The couples then weaved in and out, over and under, their hands joined like live Celtic knotwork. At one point in the set, Trout held Meg's arms and they twirled in a circle as fast and as hard as they could. For the first time ever, Meg understood why her sister loved to dance—it was exhilarating!

When they finally sat back down they were surprised to see that Alonzo Woods had joined their table, a pint of Guinness in hand.

"Hello, children," he said to Meg and Trout as they settled into their chairs. He was talking with Shay in low tones and they had very serious looks on their faces. Meg could not make out what they were saying but she could tell that her mom was uncomfortable.

"What's that about?" asked Trout.

"Maybe he's telling her how he found us out at the castle in the fog, and my mom is mad that I was out on the water after my accident," she whispered back.

Shay and Mr. Woods continued their discussion in hushed tones. When he finished his drink he stood up and went back to the bar.

Shay looked over to Meg. "I need to talk to you." She got up from the table, took Meg by the hand, and walked her outside.

Meg was nervous and started to speak before her mom did. "I'm sorry, Mom. We were careful on the water and Trout knew exactly what he was doing."

"What are you talking about?"

"Us rowing out to the castle in the fog yesterday. I just had to get out there and I forced Trout to take me."

"Oh, that…" Shay said, giving Meg a look and a nod. "I knew about that already. Declan called me after he gave you two the currach."

Meg was relieved, but now curious. "Then why did you bring me out here?"

"Mr. Woods wants to buy Owen's property."

"What!"

"He's an archeologist who does a lot of research on Bofin and he wants a permanent base here."

"No. Mom, we can't sell it. It's ours."

"Meg, it's actually Nanny's, so it will be up to her to decide what to do with it. Besides, what can we do with property in Ireland?"

Like a sudden storm, Meg burst out and told her mother about her discovery and all that had gone on the day before.

"Granuaile…," a smile crossed Shays lips. "I suppose it's possible. Do you know she has direct descendants in Westport Sligo that trace their lineage all the way back to her son Tibbot?"

Meg nodded her head. "She also had three children with her first husband, Donal O'Flaherty. Maybe we come from one of them. Why else would they put on the white sails of a king for Owen today?"

"Hereditary kings don't exist anymore in Ireland. 'Kings,'" Shay made air quotes with her fingers, "are chosen by people in certain areas to lead, but the title does not pass on to the king's children. Back in Cleggan, I was told that Owen was called the King of Inishark because he was the oldest one left from the island and that the remainder of the Shark islanders wanted to pay him his due respects with the white sails when they heard we had sailed up from Galway in a hooker."

Meg was unconvinced. "But we can't sell, Mommy… It's our home."

"Nanny will have to decide that for herself when we call her tomorrow. For the time being we need to get ready," she kissed Meg on the forehead. "It's Halloween and we are in Ireland, which is where the holiday first started! Let's have some fun!" Shay put her arm around Meg's shoulders and led her back into the pub.

23

Samhain in Eire

Meg and her mother spent the rest of the day at the pub. In between sets of singing and dancing Shay told Meg all about the history of Halloween in Ireland.

The American holiday of Halloween traces its roots back to the ancient Celtic celebration of *Samhain*. The Celtic year was divided into two halves based upon the path of the Sun: the light half and the dark half. The light half was called *Bealtaine* and was celebrated with the rise of the moon on the thirtieth of April. Bealtaine was dedicated to the fertility of the land and the increase in the hours of daylight as the days and weeks progressed.

Samhain, which began each year around October 30, was considered the Celtic New Year. Great bonfires were lit in celebration of the New Year, and all household fires had to be doused then relit from the Samhain bonfire. Samhain commemorated the harvest and the end of the light half of the year. It was also a time when the veil that separated this world from the otherworld—that is, the afterlife, or beyond—was very thin. It was believed that, at the time of Samhain, fairies and ghosts walked in our world along with living people. In order to confuse the spirits and keep them from doing harm, the Irish would dress up like them. Kids went door-to-door to sing songs and offer prayers for the dead in exchange for a soul cake, a flattened bread with fruit inside. These customs lead to modern-day trick-or-treating.

Meg knew most of the stuff her mom told her already but Shay was in a talkative mood and Meg didn't want to stop her. Shay's storytelling had reached a new level of enchantment in Ireland, and Meg detected a little bit of an Irish accent developing in her mom's speech the longer they were in the country. The stories eventually ended, and the Murphys and Davins left the pub.

It was dark as they stepped outside to a crystal clear night. Looking out across the water on the shores of Ireland the dark hills loomed in the distance and they could see tiny Samhain bonfires on the tops of them. To Meg they looked like dark giants with miniature crowns. The surreal scene was like something out of a fairy tale. Meg loved the idea of bonfires on Halloween and thought that next year they should have a Samhain fire of their own. Halloween had always been a favorite holiday of the Murphys. Every year they celebrated New England's beautiful fall foliage and the arrival of chilly nights with a party at their house. The whole family, including Shay and Mark, dressed in costume and went trick-or-treating until their bags were full of candy. Meg realized this was the first time in days she had thought of home. And, for the first time in her life, she was not in a rush to go back.

Meg turned and looked around Inishbofin for bonfires. Seeing none, she asked Trout why there weren't any on this side of the water. Trout reminded her that, since there were no trees on Bofin, wood was hard to come by. Before Meg could express disappointment at not being able to experience a Halloween bonfire, Trout added that he had been saving up pieces of driftwood that he had collected from along the shoreline, and that they would be able to light a pile of that when they got home. They continued their walk down the dark road under the glow of the stars. On the way, they passed a few children wearing homemade costumes going trick-or-treating from door to door.

Later that night Trout led Meg to the top of a hill where he lit his bonfire. Even though it was not as big as those Meg viewed from across the water, she was happy to be celebrating in this tradition all the same. The rest of the family had stayed at the house to take Deirdre out trick-or-treating and to tell ghost stories.

Now that they were alone, Trout took the opportunity to ask Meg, "What was that back at the pub with yer ma?"

"Mr. Woods wants to buy Owen's property from us so he can have a permanent base on Bofin."

"Really...Or maybe he knows more about Owen O'Flaherty than he let on."

"What do you mean?"

"Remember back out at the fort, The Digger said that he had been searching for the key to finding Granuaile's treasure. What if the key is buried somewhere on your property?"

"It's actually my grandmother's, not mine."

"Whatever! When Owen was alive, The Digger couldn't go on his property without permission. And I doubt he got it 'cause Owen spoke to no one. What if The Digger had been waiting for him to die so he could look for the key? Isn't it funny how he just happened to be going up the coast at the same time as the two of you?"

"I don't know. Maybe. How do we find out what he's up to?"

"Let's sneak onto his boat to see if we can figure it out. When he is here, The Digger usually stays at the pub until late, so we should have some time."

"Let's do it!"

Meg couldn't believe what she had just agreed to do, but the thought of finding out more about her ancestor's treasure overcame her anxiety about sneaking onto someone else's boat at night. Trout stomped out his tiny fire and they walked down the hill making their way towards the harbor. A couple of times they were frightened by other kids who jumped out from behind walls and yelled "Boo!", putting them more on edge than they already were.

From the beach where the Davin's currach lay, they could see that Alonzo's skiff was still tied up to the pier. They carefully turned the boat over and dragged it down to the water.

Slowly Trout and Meg rowed out to the large motor yacht, pausing a couple of times to make sure the coast was clear. Meg's senses were all on high alert; she thought she might be able to hear a conversation going on in Cleggan if she tried. And with every splash of the oars, she thought they would be alerting anyone on the shore to their mission. But they reached the yacht unnoticed. They tied the currach up to the far side so that it could not be seen from the town and carefully climbed on board.

The moon had risen and the night was lit with its eerie glow. Meg reached out and turned the handle of the door to the cabin which, to her relief, was unlocked. Like a pair of cat burglars she and Trout crept inside. They entered into a galley and dining room area. Meg could see on the far bulkhead, securely held in place with special straps, a large library of books on a shelf. Just below, there was a table for eating. Meg noticed there was a newspaper on the table.

She walked over and pointed to an article on the opened page, "Look at this."

"The death notice," Trout said.

Meg read aloud. "Inishbofin. Mr. Owen O'Flaherty, originally from Inishark Galway, was found last evening by his neighbors at his home on Inishbofin. He is survived by a daughter, Kathleen, who lives in the United States. There are no funeral arrangements at this time."

"He was coming here on purpose!"

"I wonder if he knew my mom and I were coming," Meg whispered.

"Nobody knew about you but my family," Trout replied.

They searched the titles of the books on the shelf. There were books on Granuaile, pirates, Barbary corsairs, Ireland, and many old books with no titles on the spine. Meg unstrapped the books and took down one of the old, untitled ones.

The leather binding was falling apart. She held the book delicately and opened it only to discover that it was in another language that she did not understand, so she replaced it on the shelf. None of the other books held clues that they could easily decipher, so Meg replaced the strap that held the books secure from the movement of the ocean.

"Let's check the stateroom," Meg said as she led the way down the passageway. Trout was surprised to hear her suggest that, and Meg had even surprised herself at her own daring, but there was a family treasure involved and they needed to get to the bottom of this.

Moonlight poured into the cabin through a porthole. They saw a well-made bed and looked around, but the cabin was neat and nothing was lying out in the open. On the far bulkhead wall they saw a door to what they thought was a closet. Upon opening the door they discovered a large safe inside. The door to the safe was slightly ajar. Meg swung open the heavy door, revealing a small, leather-wrapped package amidst a pile of old-looking scrolls. The package was worn and tied up with a strap. Meg carefully untied the strap. Inside the oiled skin was a small book. Like the wrapping, the book was very old. They were disappointed to find the handwritten words on the inside were also in another language. Meg turned the pages that were covered in writing and drawings.

"That's Bofin!" Trout said, pointing to a hand-drawn map of the island. It showed the harbor with a line across the mouth. Written in the space under where the ruins would be located, they read *Castillo Bosco* and on the other side *Castillo Grania*.

"*Castillo*…" Meg had just started to take Spanish classes in school. "*Castle*, that's castle in Spanish. Bosco's Castle! I wish I paid more attention in class so I could read the rest. Do you know Spanish?"

"I barely speak English!" Trout joked.

Towards the back of the book they saw the phrase **Bruja del Mar** in heavy bold writing, repeated over and over.

"The Digger called Granuaile *bruja*, witch. This must be the diary of Don Bosco!"

The quiet sound of the water against the hull was suddenly broken by the growl of an outboard motor being started across the harbor. Meg and Trout looked out the porthole and much to their horror saw Mr. Woods making his way across the water towards his yacht. Meg quickly rewrapped the diary and placed it back in the safe. They rushed back up the passageway but it was too late. By the time they got out the door and started to get back in the currach, Alonzo Woods had already seen them. While they stood on the aft deck of his yacht waiting to be busted, Meg looked down to the *Cailín Mo Chroí* that was still tied up to the side and came up with a plan. Al tied up his skiff and climbed onto the deck.

"Happy Halloween, children... My boat is a little out of the way to go trick-or-treating, don't you think?" Alonzo said in a very serious tone. His speech was slurred.

"Mr. Woods! Perfect timing. Trout here brought me out to our boat to get something I left onboard." Meg pulled on the chain around her neck and showed him the compendium that was underneath her shirt.

Alonzo's eyes lit up as he saw it. "What is that?" he said. Meg knew he was pretending to not know what it was.

"It's just a gift my grandmother gave me for my birthday. It's an..."

"Astronomical compendium," Alonzo finished.

"You know about them? Well, I was back on the island trying to explain to Trout how my mother and I know how to navigate by the stars, and realized I left it on the *Cailín Mo Chroí*, so we came out to get it."

"You left it on the boat?" Alonzo said, unbelieving.

"I had put it in a safe place when we left Galway and I just remembered about it when I was talking to Trout. Not too many people know what this is. How do you know about it?"

"Come, let me show you something," he said, leading them back into the yacht. Trout gave Meg a worried look when Alonzo turned his back on them. Alonzo turned on the cabin light and told them to sit them down at the table. Before they did, however, he grabbed the newspaper that was on it and took it with him into his stateroom. He returned with the leather-wrapped package that Meg had just placed back into the safe just moments before.

"This is something my grandfather gave me," he said, revealing the book. "It's the log book of Alonzo Bosco. It has been in my family for generations."

"How did your family get it?" asked Meg.

"Alonzo Bosco is my ancestor."

"But your name is Woods."

"It was a common thing to Anglicize foreign names. You know, make them sound more English. Bosco, or *bosque* in Spanish, is translated to *forest* in English, or *woods*, just like *Grania Ni Mallie* is Grace O'Malley in English. When the *Bruja del Mar*, or, *witch of the sea*, chased Don Bosco off Inishbofin he went back to our home in Spain. That is where my family has been ever since."

Alonzo opened the log book to a page and read. "I intercepted a galley bound for the Sea Witch today and found a letter on board from a map maker in London. He is writing to tell her that he has accepted her commission and will begin working on her special map in earnest. He has given no details of what he is making for her but the letter is signed by a Humphrey Cole. I wonder if the Sea Witch has commissioned a map to my treasure! Her treachery knows no ends!" Alonzo finished reading and closed the log book. "Not only did Humphrey Cole make maps, he was one of the greatest instrument makers in Elizabethan England." He looked at the compendium hanging around Meg's neck.

Meg instinctively brought her hand up as if protecting the compendium. She put it back inside her shirt.

"Wow! That sure is cool. You are related to a pirate."

"As are you," Alonzo said, squinting at her.

Meg feigned surprise. "I don't know what you are talking about. But it's late and Trout and I have to get back now," she said as she took Trout by the hand and led him towards the door.

"Yes. Yes, it is late and you must get back to your mother," Alonzo's face was cold as ice. He followed them out and watched as they boarded the currach. "Could you do something for me?"

"Sure, Mr. Woods. Anything."

"Tell your mother that the deal is off. I have no use for your land anymore."

Alonzo Woods stood like a statue on the deck of his boat and watched them row their way back to shore. They pulled the currach up on the beach, turned it over, and ran all the way back to the West Quarter under the Halloween moon. Meg glanced back once and saw Alonzo still standing where they had left him on the aft deck of his boat.

When they reached Owen's cottage Trout said, "What are you going to do? It's obvious the compendium is the key he was after. I thought he was gonna snatch it off yer neck!"

"I'm not sure, but I've got to tell my mom about all of this." She looked inside the door of the cottage and saw her mother sleeping on the bed with a turf fire burning in the fireplace. Meg closed the door and turned to Trout. "I can't believe it. She is sleeping!"

"I can't say that I blame her. She was up early with the ferry from Cleggan, and it has been a very long day for the two of yas."

Meg nodded in agreement.

"You were brilliant back there with the whole story ya told," Trout said to Meg with a big smile.

"It came to me in a flash. I even surprised myself as the words came out of my mouth!" She smiled back.

"Good luck with tellin yer ma," Trout said as he walked back towards his house. "I'll see ya in the morning."

Meg watched Trout walk across the road, and then went into Owen's cottage. Shay briefly woke when she entered and smiled at her saying, "Oh, good, you're home finally." She fell right back to sleep as Meg slipped into bed next to her. Meg, too, fell asleep quickly despite her racing thoughts.

24

Bad Tidings

Surprisingly, Meg woke up early the next morning, even before her mother did. She decided to take a walk to sort things out in her head before she would have to tell her mom what had happened the night before.

It was another grey day outside and raining lightly as Meg walked down the road. She decided that, instead of heading in her usual direction toward the harbor, she would go in the opposite direction to the west. Before pulling up her hood, she took the compendium off to look at it again—this time with the newfound knowledge that it somehow held the key to finding a treasure. She studied it even more carefully than she had previously.

Meg did not think that the front of the compendium, with its engraved *G* and Celtic art, could really hide any clues. She looked more closely and, apart from the knotwork and strange beasts, there were no hidden letters or numbers that she could tell, even when she turned it upside down or sideways. The back had just a woman's face with hair radiating in all directions. The only difference from the front was that it was not engraved on the surface of the metal; it was a relief, as if it was stamped and raised like the face on a coin. Again, there was nothing obvious about the woman's hair or face that could be a clue or a map. Meg stared at the woman. *It must be Grania,* she thought.

Meg next opened the compendium to look at the inner leafs. Although she did not fully understand what each of the instruments did, she knew from the lesson her mother had given her on the Aran Islands, that one was a volvelle. She kind of remembered how to use it. Upon closer inspection, she saw the initials *H. C.* engraved in the center of the discs of the volvelle. *That must be Humphrey Cole*, she thought, *the guy Alonzo said was commissioned by Granuaile to make the map.* Now that she had found the initials of the man mentioned in Don Bosco's log, she was even more convinced that her compendium held the key to finding the treasure. She kept examining.

She looked at the tools one by one. There was the fold-out sundial for telling time in the daylight. Next was something her mom had called an astrolabe, for determining elevations of the sun or stars. The list of ports with their coordinates was unremarkable; she again recognized *Gaillimh* but she now also recognized *Inis Bó Finne*. She saw a few other names of *Inishes*, that is, islands, but did not know them. She would have to translate all of the names and locate the places on a map later on, to see if there was any clue.

Meg looked up and realized she had walked quite a long distance. She was on a part of the island she had not been to before. Across a few fields she saw a pond. On the shore of the pond she saw an old woman walking along with a white cow. She thought it was quite interesting, as she was on the island of the "white cow." It was just like the story of how the island was founded. Before turning around and heading back, she decided she would have to ask Trout who it was who actually owned the white cow.

On her way back, Meg continued to examine every symbol and every detail that she recognized both on and inside the compendium, but there was no map. Since her mom knew what every instrument inside the compendium did, she was going to have to help her figure it out.

The sweet smell of turf fires hung in the air. As Meg approached Owen's cottage she saw smoke coming from the chimney. Her mom was up.

"Hi, Mom," Meg said as she walked through the door. Shay was putting a brick of turf on the fire.

"I was wondering where you were…I figured you ran off with your new boyfriend, Trout, again."

Meg blushed. "He is not my boyfriend, Mom! I just went for a walk to see more of the island and to think about things."

"Oh, the deep thoughts of an eleven-year-old… But now, since you're here, why don't we walk down to the hotel for breakfast again."

"Sounds great. I'm starving."

They left the house and headed back towards the harbor to where the hotel was. The clouds passed quickly overhead and Meg told her mom about everything that had happened the night before. She even confessed the part about her and Trout breaking into Mr. Woods's boat.

"This is quite an amazing yarn you're spinning, Meg. So, you are telling me that Mr. Woods, who helped save your life, is the descendant of the corsair Don Bosco, and has an evil plan to find the treasure of Granuaile that is buried somewhere on our family's land?"

"The treasure isn't buried on our land, Mom. The key is… Well, not exactly, the key is around my neck."

"So you found a key, did you?"

"I didn't find it. Nanny gave it to me," Meg said, pulling the compendium out from under her shirt.

"Oh, the old compendium is a key to a treasure now. I always thought it was a treasure in and of itself."

"Stop patronizing me, Mom. This is real and I need your help. Mr. Woods knows it's the key. In fact, once he saw that I had it, he told me to tell you the deal is off!"

"What?" Meg's mother was clearly upset. "Margaret Grace Murphy, we are going to find Mr. Woods and you are going to apologize to him. And I am going to try and save what would have been a great deal of money for your grandmother." Shay Murphy gave her daughter a stern look. They rounded the corner of the road that led down to the harbor. At that very moment, they both looked out to see that Al Wood's big motor yacht was gone. The *Cailín Mo Chroí* was still there, but tied to the mooring it once shared with Mr. Woods's boat.

"Great," her mom said, exasperated. "He's gone. You have really done it this time, sister! I don't know what has gotten into you since we've been in Ireland, but it is going to stop once we get back home. All of this sneaking out and doing bad things to people is un-ac-ceptable." Meg knew she was in deep trouble whenever her mother said words in distinct syllables.

Mother and daughter sat in silence at the hotel while they ate breakfast. Occasionally Shay would shake her head, as if she was having a conversation with herself. When they finished eating, she went to use the phone to call back to America, and Meg walked sullenly down to the beach in the harbor, where she found Trout with his dad and brother mending lobster pots.

"How'd it go?" Trout asked her.

"Not well. Can you believe he is gone?" Meg said, motioning to the mooring where the yacht was.

"The Digger must've left last night, 'cause we've been here since dawn and there was no trace of him or his boat."

"My mom is really mad at me for breaking into his boat and ruining the deal he had offered to buy the cottage."

"Ehh, she'll get over it."

"I hope so. I also hope she lets me hang out with you for the rest of the time we're here. When I got back from a walk I took in the early morning, she called you my boyfriend," Meg said with a sheepish grin.

Trout's face turned a brighter shade of red than it usually was, and he tried to change the subject. "When're ya leavin'?"

"We're flying out tomorrow night, so I wonder if we are leaving here today to return the hooker."

Shay walked up to Meg and Trout as they were talking. She said hello to Declan and Dennis, and then turned to talk to Meg. She surprisingly looked relieved and said to her, "You're off the hook, Meg. You're nanny would not have sold the land to anyone, let alone to a Barbary corsair." She smiled and looked at the two of them. "We are going to have to leave soon, so why don't you and Trout go spend some time together while I pack up. But don't get into trouble this time, okay?" she said with a wink.

25

Saint Colman's Monastery

Trout asked permission from his dad to go off with Meg. He agreed and soon they were walking off in the only direction they had not yet traveled together on the island, east.

They took the low road again and eventually wound their way on it up another hill. Down below they could see the inner harbor where a few boats were moored. The wreck of an old fishing boat sat on the shores, rusting away. Trout pointed out the ruins of the old fish curing house on an island opposite an old pier. Beyond that was the rocky hill that eventually led out to where the castle was. The sun peeked its light and warmth from behind some clouds as they looked down to a large field and a beach in the distance. Off to the north, beyond the far beach, there was another island that Trout said was called Inishturk, which meant the 'island of the wild boar,' but the Bofin islanders called it Boar Island, and the Boar islanders, in turn, called Bofin, Cow Island. "They're the boars and we're the cows!" Trout said with a laugh.

"You cow," Meg teased. "Oh yeah, I forgot to tell you that when I took that walk this morning I saw a woman by the pond walking a white cow like in the story. I thought it was great. Does she do it for the tourists?"

The color drained completely from Trout's face. Meg asked him what was wrong.

"That's bad. That's really bad. I guess I forgot to tell you the other part of the legend of Bofin. That pond, as you call it, is *Lough Bo Finne*. It is said that when something really bad is about to happen, the cow or the woman emerge near it to forewarn the islanders. They have shown up to warn of bad storms and deaths, but no matter what, when the white cow and woman are seen, something bad is going to happen."

Meg and Trout both looked off into the distance as if they could see the approach of bad weather.

"Maybe we shouldn't sail back to Galway today."

"I'd say that probably wouldn't be a bad idea. But the storm's not upon us yet, so let's keep going." Trout's worried look slowly went away and he said, "You're going to love the ruins of the old abbey."

They walked a bit further down the road, past a small lily pond, to a ruin that looked to be only about the size of a cottage. It was surrounded by old and new gravestones. Coming down from the road, they entered the roofless church through a small door. This church was about the same size as St. Leo's on Shark Island. Trout had Meg sit down in the center. At the far end of the ruins he climbed up onto a stone bench located under what was once a window.

"Now, sit there, Megeen, and let me tell ye the story of Inishbofin's patron saint. In the seventh century, Saint Colman was an Irish monk on the English island of Iona. He was very smart and virtuous, and was made the Bishop of Lindisfarne, another English island. He was called to represent the Celtic custom of Easter at the Synod of

Whitby, against the Roman way that was becoming the norm in southern England."

"What's the Synod of Whitby?"

"I haven't a stinkin' clue. Just listen to the story." Trout twirled his hands like an actor taking a bow, "Anyway, so they had decided at this Synod to get rid of the Celtic way and Saint Colman was pretty pissed off about that. He stormed out and left England to come back home to Ireland where they celebrated Easter the right way. He even had a few monks follow him, both English and Irish. They set up an abbey here and were soon getting back to their *monk-ey* business." At that, he gave a little wink and Meg laughed.

"Now, the Irish monks came back to their home, you see, so they had a lot of family and friends to visit. They left the English ones here to do the work of building the abbey while they went out to have some *craic*."

"Crack? What in the world are you talking about?"

"I forgot, you Yanks don't know about the craic. Craic means *fun* in Irish." Meg smiled with approval. "Since the Irish monks kept going out for the craic, the English ones got real mad and demanded Saint Colman take them off this island and set up a separate English monastery on the mainland in Mayo, which he did. The Irish monks continued on happily here, and it was the first time the English were chased off Inishbofin and long before the great Granuaile chased off that stupid Spaniard, Don Bosco. And that is the end of me tale," Trout said as he took a big bow.

Meg clapped her hands and laughed with delight at Trout's theatrics. A moment later, they heard the sound of someone else applauding, too. Meg and Trout both turned and saw Alonzo Woods entering the ruins.

"Bravo," he said from the entrance. "Quite a good story, and very close to the truth. I just wish you had not offended my ancestor at the end."

Meg jumped up and ran towards Trout. "We thought you left Bofin," she said.

"Why would I leave when I just discovered the key to the treasure? I only moved my boat to the other side of the island to follow a clue I discovered in an old scroll."

Although she did not really trust him, the mention of a clue to the treasure piqued Meg's interest. "What clue did you discover, Mr. Woods?"

"Why don't the two of you follow me so I can show you for yourselves?"

"Before we go anywhere, why don't you tell us exactly where you want us to go?" Trout said with all the bravado he could muster.

"There was an old scroll I had found a while ago that I reread after we talked last night. It was another message intercepted by Don Bosco on its way to the Sea Witch. It read, 'Where *Mananann MacLir* blows his nose, at noon, the bronze circle shows, the way to the bald queen's treasure.' I never knew what the bronze circle was until I saw the compendium last night. You still have it with you, I suppose?"

Meg put her hand to the spot where it was under her shirt and nodded.

Trout spoke to Meg, "*Mananann MacLir* was the Irish God of the Sea." Replaying the words from the message,

Trout muttered under his breath, "Where the sea god blows his nose…the blowhole!"

"What's the blowhole?" Meg asked.

"In geology a blowhole is formed when an underwater cave grows into the land. It continues to grow upward as water erodes the land, until it opens back up on the surface," Alonzo said.

"Yeah, we have one here, but it's back down the west."

"What time is it?"

"It's after ten. I'm not sure if we can get there and back before noon, and don't you have to leave to get back to America then?" Trout said, trying to steer Meg away from the idea of heading off with Alonzo.

"America will have to wait. We have a pirate treasure to find!"

"What about yer ma?"

"Like you said before, Trout, she'll get over it."

"Yes, she'll get over it. I actually have a vehicle up on the high road, but we must hurry," Alonzo said as he led them out of the abbey.

26

The Grotto

Alonzo raced up the hill that separated the low road from the high road. Meg and Trout were not far behind. Along the way, Meg and Trout were able to whisper back and forth without Alonzo hearing them.

"How did he know we were at the abbey?"

"He must've seen us from the high road and come down. I'm gettin' sick of him creeping up on us all of the time." Trout looked up and stuck his tongue out behind Alonzo's back.

"Yeah, I know, but he wants to bring us along to find the treasure."

"He only wants us 'cause you have the key."

"But he has the clues, and without him we wouldn't know anything about the treasure."

"True enough. But I still don't trust him. He's slimy as an eel."

Sitting at the high road, as promised, was a beat up, old land rover. They got inside and soon Al was driving them uncomfortably fast down the narrow road, heading west. A few times along the way they were forced to wait until a cow or sheep cleared off the roadway, but they soon passed the pond where Meg had seen the woman with the white cow. They drove past the beach on the bay where they saw Mr. Woods's yacht anchored.

"I have always thought that the Sea Witch hid the treasure in a sea cave because she knew these islands better than anyone. I have even searched the blowhole in the past. Is there anything on the compendium that might help us?" Alonzo asked Meg.

"I really am not sure. There are all sorts of things in it and I barely know how to use any of them," Meg replied.

"I know that, once a day, the sun comes straight down into the grotto for just a short time," Trout added, using the name the locals called the blowhole.

"There is a sundial. That must be what we need to use."

"Ah, a sundial. That sounds very promising. We may just find the treasure after all," Alonzo said. He pulled the land rover off the road and stopped alongside a well-worn path that headed towards the ocean.

The three walked down the path and soon found themselves under the earth in a rocky cave that had been carved out from millions of years of the violent Atlantic Ocean hitting rock. The echoing sound of waves through the ancient cave was like nothing Meg had ever heard; it was very haunting. The cave had the interesting smell of both deep earth and the sea. Meg looked down past misty rocks where the sun had just begun to shine its light, and there, just below them, a seal was poking its head out of the turquoise water. It had dark gray skin and strange, cloudy white eyes that seemed to be looking straight at her. Meg nudged Trout.

"Look at that," she pointed to the seal.

"There is a large seal colony just outside this cave. That one must have cataracts," Alonzo chimed in.

The seal did not shy away. It remained there, looking directly at them. Meg was convinced the seal was her great grandmother, the selkie who had saved her.

As if reading Meg's mind, Trout whispered to her, "There she is. She's watching over you again."

"Would you let me have the compendium?" Alonzo asked Meg.

She pulled the chain and brought it out of her shirt. Not taking it off her neck, she said, "You can look, but you can't touch. It's my family's treasure."

She held up the compendium for Alonzo to see. His mouth gaped open. "It is much more exquisite than I imagined. Can you open it, please?"

The light of the sun reflected brightly off the metal. Meg pressed the latch and exposed the inner instruments. She carefully opened up the small sundial that was on hinges. The circular dial opened on top of a semicircular base. Attached to the base was a long, pointed needle that folded out to protrude past the dial. They looked at the markings, but other than the roman numerals representing the hours, there was nothing else remarkable about the sundial.

"Maybe this is the wrong tool," Meg said.

"No. You need to hold it in the right place." Alonzo reached out to grab it, but Meg pulled it back towards her.

"What do you mean?"

He nudged Meg and Trout further down into the cave until they were standing on the last rock before the water. "You must hold it above your head facing the western ocean at exactly noon, and the reflection will show us where to look. It's almost noon now. Do it!" Alonzo yelled.

Meg looked at Trout. She pulled the chain over her head and held the compendium as high as she could. The sun glinted off the metal in an indiscernible spattering of light on the walls of the cave. Meg looked all around her but was unable to see anything specific being lit up. Alonzo was standing behind Meg. Just as she was about to turn to ask him what to look for, he grabbed the compendium and thrust both her and Trout into the water.

The water was cold, but the shock of what Alonzo had just done brought Meg to the reality of the situation. When she came up, she saw him running out of the cave at top speed.

"What are you doing?" she screamed to him as he retreated ever further.

"You stupid kids! Do you really think I would show you how to find my treasure?"

His voice echoed down the blowhole and out to the ocean. Meg began to drag herself out of the water when she realized Trout wasn't next to her. She turned and saw him flailing his arms, struggling to keep from drowning. She quickly dove back into the water and pulled him up on the rocks.

Trout had a look of terror on his face. He coughed violently, spitting out water and gasping for breath.

"You don't know how to swim?" Meg yelled at him.

Trout looked at her, annoyed at her question, "Of course I don't, or I would've saved meself!" he said between coughs.

Meg started up the cave. "We've got to get my treasure back." Trout recovered and followed close behind. They ran as fast as they could, but when they got back to the road, all they saw was dust kicking up farther down as Alonzo raced his land rover for his yacht.

"We'll never get it now," Meg said disheartened.

"We have one chance. Me da usually is lobstering in a cove on the other side of this hill. If he's there, maybe we can intercept The Digger before he gets out of the bay," Trout said, pointing to the rocky hill behind them.

"How are we going to catch him in a row boat?"

"The tourists are gone! Da put the outboard on the currach this morning!"

Meg didn't even hesitate. She took off in a run towards the hill with her friend by her side.

27

The Chase

Not far into their run, Meg's heart started to race and she was losing her breath. Even though the incline on the hill was not very steep, Meg wheezed and she was not sure she would be able to make it to the top. The farthest distance Meg had ever run before was out to the dock and into the water back at home. Her premature birth had left her with weaker than normal lungs and even the short run to the dock always winded her. As she struggled to breathe, she thought back to what had just happened. How could she have been so gullible? Trout had told her more than once to not trust that nasty man, but curiosity got the best of her. Alonzo's echoing voice was stuck in her head. *Stupid kids. Do you really think I would help you find my treasure!* But just the thought of him getting away gave Meg the strength she needed, and she was able to catch her breath and run like she had never run before.

The road led Meg and Trout up past bogs and then down towards rocky cliffs. They finally reached the edge of the island. In the distance, Meg saw several large, stone outcroppings and beyond, lonely Shark Island. When they looked down to the water, the welcome sight of Trout's father and brother greeted them. The two were dressed in yellow fishing gear and standing in the currach in the middle of the cove. As they made their way down the rocks Trout whistled. His father looked up and waved to Trout and Meg. He then started his outboard motor and pulled the boat up to them.

"I'm asking meself, 'Why it is Megeen and you, who were headed to the east, are now in the west quarter whistling for me when she should be headin' back to Galway?'"

"Da, the Digger tricked us and stole Granuaile's compendium from Meg. He's around in the bay and gonna be headed out right now if we don't stop him."

Trout's father looked back and forth at the two desperate kids and an incredulous grin spread across his weather-beaten face. "Well, it's a good thing I put the outboard on, isn't it." Declan reached out and helped Meg and Trout get in the currach. "What about yer vow, Megeen?"

Although it was the last thing on her mind, she instantly said, "My vow is to stay off a motor boat. This currach is a rowboat with a motor on it...big difference. Just get me to that yacht!"

Declan twisted the handle of the outboard. The motor growled back, and soon they were darting across the waves faster than Meg could have imagined. Dozens of seals occupied the cove, but despite the speed of the currach and the sound of the motor as it passed through the cove, not one budged an inch. Meg looked around to see if she could find the seal she had seen earlier in the grotto—the one with the cloudy white eyes—but that seal was nowhere to be found. Meg felt certain she would recognize her great grandmother again by those eyes.

The sea water crashed over the bow of the currach as they raced around the point. Meg was both thrilled and sad at the same time: thrilled, because she had never been on a boat going as fast as the currach was at that moment, and sad because she had lived with her vow for so long and now it was broken. The boat skipped up and down in the rolling ocean. It soon passed the entrance to the blowhole and the grotto. At one point Dennis handed Meg a plastic bowl amid the sea spray raining down all over them.

"What's this for?" she asked.

"For you to bail the boat out with," he said matter-of-factly.

Meg immediately started scooping out the water that was collecting in the hull of the currach. It did not take long before they saw Alonzo's yacht ahead of them, making its way north towards Boar Island.

"There it is. We'll be on it soon. What'll ya do when we get to it?" Trout asked Meg.

"Board it, of course. I am a pirate princess, you know."

"We're gonna need these." Trout handed her a fishing knife that was under the seat and took one for himself.

Declan looked at Meg and Trout. He smiled, shook his head in disbelief, and then, in a jerking move of his chin toward Meg, shouted to Dennis, "O'Flahertys!" But he kept the currach on course.

Fortunately, the yacht was moving as slowly as a whale and they gained on it very quickly. They did not see Alonzo anywhere on the decks of the yacht and figured he must have been in the pilot house. Declan pulled the currach alongside the yacht, and Meg and Trout jumped on the aft deck.

Trout's brother tried to grab hold of the hull but they were crashing over big waves which made that impossible. He and Declan were forced to pull behind and follow the yacht.

From the moment they stepped on board, Meg's heart was pounding in her chest like a drum and she seriously thought the sound of it would give them away. They were unable to see inside the tinted windows of the yacht as they crept their way towards the door. Meg reached out her hand and turned the knob to the galley door and slowly pulled it open. Alonzo was not inside. The table was covered with scrolls, and books had spilled out from the shelf, the strap that normally held them just dangling. Meg held her finger to her lips to signal for Trout to be quiet as they tiptoed into the cabin. She could hear nothing over the hum of the engines and the waves crashing into the hull. Trout pointed up a ladder to the pilot house and whispered in her ear, "He must be up there."

Meg stepped closer to the table. Amid all the scattered papers she saw the diary of Don Bosco wrapped tightly in its leather cover. Impulsively she grabbed it and tucked it into her pants. *Steal from me; I'll steal from you*, she thought.

"He may have the compendium on him," she whispered to Trout, "but let's check the safe anyway."

They snuck down the hallway and opened the door to the stateroom. Meg was practically expecting Alonzo to spring out from behind something, but he was not there either. She went straight to the safe they had found open the night before, and turned the handle again.

"He really should lock this thing." She pulled the heavy door open. Her heart skipped a beat when she saw light reflecting off the brassy, haunting gaze of Grace O'Malley's image on the compendium. She was never so glad to see anything in her life. She grabbed it, and then she and Trout headed back out the way they had come in. Alonzo was still nowhere to be found. They easily walked back out on the aft deck of the yacht, waving for Declan to come back aside them.

"You little *bruja*! You don't give up do you," yelled Alonzo as he clambered down a ladder from above. When he got to the deck, Trout lunged at him with the knife. Alonzo swiftly dodged the thrust and hit Trout over the head with his fist, sending him to the deck. The knife went tumbling away from Trout, and Alonzo picked it up. Turning towards Meg, he said, "The Boscos will not lose to your family a second time." He drew closer to Meg. She had nowhere to go as she was up against the bulkhead with only the ocean behind her. She looked out to the water and was just about to jump in when Trout jumped Alonzo from behind and put him in a full nelson headlock. The knife dropped back to the ground and the two of them wrestled for control. Alonzo was much bigger, but Trout was a pretty strong kid, and managed to hold the headlock. They staggered back and forth coming close to falling off the back of the boat a couple of times when, suddenly, Alonzo bucked his back like a stallion and sent Trout over the side of the boat into the water.

"He can't swim!" Meg screamed. She quickly climbed the bulkhead to jump in after Trout. As she dove towards the water, Alonzo grabbed her hand. A bolt of pain shot through her. She felt her shoulder go out of joint, but held onto the compendium with all her strength. She was being dragged by her arm, half in the water, while Alonzo tried to pry open her fingers to get the compendium she was holding so tightly. Meg was in so much pain and was about to give up when the boat crashed over a large wave, breaking Alonzo's grasp and sending her into the ocean, surprising them both. The sudden release relaxed her own hand enough that she accidently let go, sending the compendium into the air.

Meg hit the water hard but managed to keep her head above it. She watched as the compendium flew through the air in an arc and splashed out of reach into the ocean. Without hesitation, she dove after it. One-armed and discombobulated from the struggle, she saw her treasure slowly sinking in front of her but could not swim fast enough. She kicked her legs as hard as she could and reached out with her good arm but it was all for naught. Meg's lungs burned from being deprived of oxygen and she was all but out of breath. She watched with horror as the brassy glimmer of the compendium disappeared into the dark depths of the Atlantic Ocean, and gave up hope of catching it. Resigned to the knowledge that she had lost it, she swam upwards. For a moment, she thought she saw the dark shadow of a seal dive down past her.

Meg surfaced with a gasp and floated on the waves with what felt like a hole in her heart. What had previously filled that hole was slowly drifting to a watery grave. She bobbed in the waves of the cold Atlantic, just as she had a few days earlier. She did not like the sensation, but she could see the dark hull of the currach against the green of the sea, and was not afraid. And this time, she was not being swept away in a current. Meg treaded water, and watched Declan and Dennis pull Trout into their boat. Alonzo's yacht was getting away but she did not care. Alonzo did not matter to her anymore. What really mattered was the she had lost Granuaile's compendium forever. Meg was devastated.

Rising up and down in the swells of the ocean, Meg started to cry. She looked to the sky and said, "I'm so very, very sorry, Grace." She blinked away her tears. Then, out of the corner of her eye, she saw something else in the water with her. She spun around and there, barely ten feet away, was the seal from the grotto, staring directly at her.

"Hello," she said to her selkie great grandmother. She was hoping she might see a glint of chain hanging from her mouth, but saw nothing. With its head just sticking out of the water, the seal remained motionless, staring at Meg with its foggy white eyes. Meg and the seal stared at each other in silence for what seemed to be a long time. The seal swam slowly towards her and stopped just a few feet away. Meg felt a tingling in her shoulder that had been hurt, and miraculously she was able to move it. She smiled at the seal and was sure it smiled back. Then, from behind, Meg heard the engine of the currach approaching. Upon hearing the boat, the selkie moved as if to dip below the surface. Before going under, Meg called out to it, "Thank you...for everything." The seal winked one white eye at her and then disappeared beneath the waves.

Declan and Dennis hauled Meg into the boat where she saw an unconscious Trout laying on the deck.

28

Things Lost

Meg performed CPR on Trout while his father rushed the currach back to shore. Trout was not responding to anything, and Meg was distraught at the thought that she might lose her first real friend. She continued to give him breaths and pump his heart. Finally, as they neared the beach, Trout coughed up some water and began to breathe again. Declan drove the currach at full speed right up the sandy beach of the eastern village Meg had seen from afar earlier in the day. He carried Trout up to the road. Fortunately, just then an islander was driving by in a rusted pickup truck. At the sight of the beached currach, the driver of the truck stopped. Declan loaded Trout in the back and they sped off.

Meg stood in the surf along with Dennis holding onto the side of the currach and praying for Trout. Meg's mother, who had been in the village looking for her and Trout, came running at the sight of a soaking wet Meg on the beach.

"Oh, my God, what happened?" Shay said as she took Meg in her arms.

"Trout drowned," was all Meg could say before she started to cry.

Shay held Meg tightly. Mother and daughter stood together on the beach, waves rolling over their feet, for a full minute.

"We have to get to him," Meg said.

Dennis said they could get back to the harbor more quickly by boat than on land. Shay agreed, and together they walked the currach back into the water. They all got on board.

They cruised in silence around the hilly peninsula that led from the island to Cromwell's fort. While they were pulling into the harbor Meg looked over to the ruins and everything she had been through in the past week flashed through her memory. She looked up to her mother with tears streaming down her cheeks and confessed, "I lost our compendium."

Shay hugged Meg tightly and said, "You can tell me about that later. For now, let's hope your friend is all right."

Some fisherman greeted them at the pier in the harbor and told them the island's nurse had checked Trout out and that he was all right. Declan had already taken him back home. The CPR Meg had performed on Trout in the currach had saved his life. Dennis hugged Meg and said she was a hero, but Meg didn't feel like one. Trout had nearly drowned because of her, and at the end of it all, they didn't even rescue the compendium.

Dennis had to unload the currach, so Shay and Meg left him to go check on Trout. While they walked up the low road back towards the west quarter, Meg filled her mother in on all of the details of what had happened. Shay listened to the story, not saying a word and feeling sad for what Meg had been through. The day had cleared up and the sun was shining. It warmed Meg's skin and worked on drying out the wet clothes that had only now started to annoy her. The smoke streaming up from the chimney of the Davin's cottage was visible from the road.

Trout's mother and father were outside talking to a neighbor. "Here is my hero!" Nell called out when she saw Meg and Shay approach. She rushed up to Meg and gave her a big hug.

"Trout is the hero," Meg said. "He was trying to save me when he was thrown overboard. I'm so sorry! It's all my fault."

Declan dismissed her with a shush. "Ah, Megeen, we've never seen Trout as happy as he has been since ya got here. Ye were only trying to save Granuaile's treasure from that nasty man. I don't blame ya at all. Trout's inside waiting for ya. Why don't ya go in and see him?"

Shay remained outside while Meg went in to see Trout, who was lying on the couch under some covers.

When Trout saw Meg enter the cottage, he laughed and said, in his awful American accent, "Excuse me. They told me you saved me."

"No, you saved me, Trout. Who knows what Alonzo would have done to me to get the compendium back!"

"Do ya still have it?" Trout said with his eyebrows arched. He nodded his head hoping for a positive response.

"It's lost in the Atlantic."

"Maybe we'll find it someday?"

"Maybe… but I doubt it." Meg was despondent.

"*She* will help ya find it."

"She?"

"Your great grandmother, of course. She was out there with us."

"How do you know about that?"

"Cause she saved me before you did." Trout smiled wide, "I was sinking like a rock and the selkie came up under me and brought me to the surface."

"Did your dad and brother see her too?" Meg asked.

"I doubt it. They probably wouldn't believe me anyway. They never do."

"I believe you, Trout... I saw her, too," Meg said seriously, looking down at him on the couch.

Then Trout remembered, "Well, what about the diary? Do ya still have that? Don't think for a minute I didn't see ya steal that off the table on The Digger's yacht."

Meg had totally forgotten about the diary. She reached behind her and, sure enough, still tucked into her wet jeans was the leather-wrapped diary of Don Bosco. She pulled it out and saw the covering was completely wet. But, when she removed the leather wrapping, she was amazed to find that the book itself was bone dry. She looked at Trout and flipped the pages to show him.

"We beat the Digger!" Trout said.

"I would pay to see the look on his face when he realizes it's gone! Do you think he'll come after me?"

"I don't know. But I'm sure he won't rest until he gets even with the 'Pirate Princess,'" Trout said with a devilish smile.

"I am not a pirate!" Meg shook her finger at her friend. "But I am a princess...It's all about perspective, ya know," Meg said in her best Irish accent. At that, they had a big laugh.

"I have to admit that you were quite the swashbuckling hero on the deck, Trout. Alonzo was twice your size and you handled him pretty well."

Trout blushed, his red cheeks a good sign he had recovered, and he puffed himself up from his place on the couch. "You'd tink from all that digging he'd be a little stronger, but he was soft as a squid... I'll tell ya one thing, though. I tink it's time I learned to swim!"

Meg nodded. "Definitely. You'll never be able to dive off a ship with a dagger in your mouth like a real pirate until you do! You've got plenty of beaches here to learn at."

"What, are ya crazy?" Trout said, his face serious. "It's freezing in the ocean! I want to learn in a nice warm pool!"

Meg laughed out loud again.

Trout's parents and Shay came inside when they heard the laughter. Meg quickly tucked the diary back into her pants before anyone noticed.

"What's going on in here?" Shay asked, with a grin.

"Only us deciding that we are the sorriest excuses ever for buccaneers."

"Yeah... 'Meg the Frozen' and 'Trout the Rock of the Sea,'" he joked.

"I'm sorry to break up such a dynamic duo, but we are going to have to leave soon or we will miss our plane home," Shay said.

The Davins escorted Shay and Meg to the pier in the harbor. Since there was not enough time to sail the *Cailín Mo Chroí* back to Galway, Declan offered to take care of that for Shay. On the way to catch the ferry they learned that the IRGC, the Irish Coast Guard, had been called but, by then,

Alonzo Woods had cruised into international waters where they could not arrest him. Meg was secretly hoping they would not find Al so that she would not get in trouble herself for stealing the diary. Meg and Trout had made a pact that they would keep the diary a secret just between the two of them, and someday they would learn to read it so they could search for the treasure themselves.

The sun was still out and the wind gently blowing across Inishbofin. The water in the harbor had a grey-green look with speckles of white where small waves broke. Declan told them that the water where Meg had let go of the compendium was very deep and that it would be impossible to find it. Meg was very sad about losing the compendium, but having the diary of Don Bosco somewhat made up for that, and gave her hope that she would one day find Granuaile's treasure.

As they boarded the ferry and motored out of Inishbofin's safe harbor, Shay teased Meg, just a little, about how silly their vow had been. Shay said that the Murphy girls needed to learn to be a little more flexible when it came to certain things. Meg agreed, but said she still preferred to ride in a sailboat. She also said they should keep their vow, with only a few exceptions.

The island grew distant behind them. Meg felt sad at leaving but she knew it would not be the last time she would see Bofin and her best friend Trout. She stood at the bow of the ferry the entire ride and kept her eyes on the water for the seal with the white eyes.

The bus ride through Connemara on their way to Shannon Airport was as spectacular as Paddy said it would be, way back when they had first picked up the *Cailín Mo Chroí* in Galway. They also passed through Galway along the way. Meg felt sadder and sadder with each field and town they passed through. The short wait for their plane at the airport was torture, and she didn't even browse through the duty-free shopping area with her mother. She sat on a bench looking out the window at the Ireland she had come to know and love. Meg held on to her backpack tightly, knowing the ancient diary of a Barbary corsair was tucked away safely in the same pocket where she had previously packed the beautiful family heirloom that was now lost.

Shay told Meg to forget about doing her homework until they got home. She knew Meg was not going to be able to do anything on the flight over the Atlantic. Meg looked out the window as the airplane lifted off the runway. She cried tears as real as any she had ever shed before. She missed Ireland already and she had only just left! When the waves of the dark ocean below were no longer discernible, Meg fell asleep and did not wake until they landed.

29

Telling Nanny

The water around her had a dark, green glow from the sunlight that made its way down to the depths. Meg was exploring the ocean floor below. Occasionally a fish swam by but Meg ignored them all. Her only task was to find special bivalve mollusks with beautiful, symmetrical pink shells. Shay was somewhere off to her left doing the same thing as Meg. Having learned everything she knew about scallop diving from her mother, Meg knew exactly where to look. She was quickly becoming an expert. Every now and then, she swirled around the small amount of water she kept in her mask to clear the fog that inevitably developed on the glass when she went scuba diving.

Scallops lived in clusters, or beds, on the seafloor. They filtered the water for the small organisms they consumed. To her right, Meg saw a large bed of scallops at the base of a small, underwater hill. She wanted to point it out to her mother but saw that she was still busy, and so swam towards the bed by herself.

Meg first grabbed the bigger scallops and put them in the mesh bag that was attached to her dive belt. She knew which ones to leave behind to keep the population healthy. Their pink shells stood out like flowers against the murky, green-brown seafloor. Meg was concentrating on her work when she felt a light tap on her shoulder from behind. Before turning to see what her mother wanted, Meg finished collecting the scallops she was working on. When she twisted her body around, she saw Shay still off in the distance at the same bed she had been working in just minutes earlier. Meg turned back to her work but noticed the scallop bed was now covered by a dark shadow. She looked up and was surprised at what she saw. Hovering above the scallops, Meg saw a pair of cloudy white eyes staring directly at her. She immediately recognized them as belonging to the selkie she knew so well.

Meg froze with shock at the sight. She had been dreaming about those eyes for years, and to see them again just in front of her, gave her goose bumps under her wet suit.

"Follow me," a soft whisper echoed in Meg's mind. The seal swam off towards the shelf that bordered the deep water.

Meg shot up straight in her bed and looked all around, the whisper from her dream lingering in her head. It was morning and even Finn was staring at her, looking as if he had heard the whisper, too. The dream was so real.

"Did you hear that, Finn?" Meg asked. Her dog jumped up on the bed and licked her face. "Fiiinnnn," Meg said, pushing the dog away. She was still jet lagged from her trip. Her "internal body clock," as her mom called it, was still on Irish time. Meg got dressed and dragged herself downstairs to the kitchen where she found her mother alone. On the table was her favorite breakfast. She ate her sandwich voraciously, enjoying good, old American bacon.

"As soon as you're finished get on your dry suit so we can go to Nanny's. She can't wait to hear of your adventure."

The weather in Connecticut had turned cold in the week they were gone. After Meg's incident, Shay wasn't fooling around anymore. She told Meg they were going to be extra careful from now on and would wear dry suits when sailing in the cold. Meg nodded in understanding and finished her breakfast. She had never worn the dry suit before and worked through its stiffness as she pulled it on. When they stepped outside, the cold air stung Meg's face. She tucked her chin into the big collar of the safety suit to stay warm. They walked down to the Muirín and, in no time, had raised the sails and were underway to Wilderness Point on Fishers Island.

The calmer waters of the sound were such a stark contrast to the rough Atlantic waves they had sailed in the week before. Shay offered the tiller to Meg but she turned it down. The events of the previous week were heavy on her mind and she didn't think she could concentrate on guiding the sailboat to the landmarks they followed on each leg of the trip to her grandmother's house. Meg sat next to Shay, watching her and looking out to the beautiful landscape that was so familiar to her. In spite of her familiarity, she sensed she was somewhere else and not at home. It was a strange feeling, one she had never experienced before.

They reached the northern shore of Fishers Island in no time. After passing between the Dumpling Islands they turned towards Race Rock Light. In the distance, off the starboard side of the boat, Meg saw her dad's lobster boat. He was standing at the helm dressed in his bright orange fishing gear. With one hand on the wheel, the other was on a line hooked around his hydraulic winch and he was pulling up a trawl.

Meg had stayed up late into the night telling him about everything that happened when she was in Ireland. He was shocked and scared about her near loss at sea, but he was equally proud of the daring and courage she showed trying to save the compendium. He could not believe his little girl had the guts to chase down a fleeing yacht and board it to steal back her lost property. When he walked her to her room and tucked her in bed for the night, he said "Goodnight, Margaret Grace, my Pirate Princess." Meg smiled at him and asked if she could go out lobstering with him soon. That put the biggest smile on his face she had ever seen.

Sailing past Race Rock Light, they saw it was empty except for some birds that were sitting on the sea wall where they had seen the banshee on the day of Meg's birthday. That trip seemed like ages ago. As they neared Wilderness Point, Meg caught a whiff of the turf smoke that was rising from the chimney of Tír na nÓg. She loved the smell, and felt like she was coming home again.

Nanny was sitting inside her all-purpose room with a wool blanket over her knees, gazing at the fire, when Meg and Shay walked into her cottage. Shay had filled her mother in on most of the details of the trip over the phone, so Meg knew she would not have to tell the whole story again. But Meg felt so badly for losing their family heirloom, she wanted to come out to Nanny's to apologize in person. Nanny had told Shay over the phone that there was no need for apologies, but Meg insisted. Nanny raised her head and smiled at them when they entered the room.

Meg immediately noticed there was something different about Nanny. While she was happy to see Meg, her slate-blue eyes had lost their twinkle. Nanny looked older and more tired than she had ever looked. When she finally spoke, her voice didn't have the familiar boom Meg was used to. In a soft voice Nanny said, "Come here, girls, and sit close to Nanny."

Meg was devastated by Nanny's demeanor and started to blame herself for the transformation. Nanny noticed how her granddaughter was reacting to her appearance, and she reached out her hand for Meg to hold.

"Meg, my dear, ya have nothing to do with the current state of yer Nanny. I've done this to meself. Since yer ma called to tell me how me dear father spent his days walkin' the shores of Bofin looking for his lost daughter, I haven't been the same."

Her movements were slow and her Irish accent was more pronounced than ever. Maybe Meg's time on Bofin had caused Meg to notice the accent more, but she was sure Nanny sounded like she just got off the boat, where she never had before.

"I knew he was heartbroken at the loss of his son to the depths of the Atlantic, but I never imagined that my own departure across the ocean would break him the way it did. I am the worst daughter in the history of the world." Tears streamed down her face. Meg and Shay sobbed with her, too, and the three closed in for a hug.

"Mom, how could you have known? He wouldn't speak to you after your fight."

"I should've known, regardless. If *you* were ever to leave me forever, over some unfathomable distance, it would've broken me in two." Nanny held Shay's face in her hand. "It was me hard-headed, stubborn pride that kept me from reaching out to him. He was already broken, and I took what little he had left away from him. I'll never forgive meself."

The three, strong women of the sea sat crying together for several minutes. When they had calmed down a bit, Shay got up to fix some tea and Meg looked up at her Nanny with big, tear-filled eyes, and said, "I can't forgive myself either for losing the compendium—Granuaile's compendium. I am so sorry, Nanny."

No sooner did Meg say the name *Granuaile* then the familiar twinkle returned to her grandmother's eyes. Nanny looked at Meg with the newfound knowledge of the secret they shared.

"So ya know, do ya?" Nanny looked over at Shay. She was putting tea bags in the cups and opening a package of cookies. "I never told her because knowledge like that could ruin a child. Knowin' you're related to the most famous of all Irish women would have some rest on the laurels of the dead and never do things for themselves. I should have told her, but she never showed the gift of the O'Malleys. She could never see the storm comin', but you could. As soon as I found out that you heard that crash the night before your birthday, and then said you'd seen our banshee when the others doubted you, I knew it was you who were the next great seafaring child in the O'Malley line. That's why I gave you the compendium. It was meant to be yours, but it was only the least of the gifts that Granuaile's descendent would receive. Tell me something, Meg. Have you ever dreamt of things that came true?" Meg nodded, amazed at what her grandmother was sharing with her. "It's another side of the gift, but you have to work on it to develop it fully. I never did, because I left my mother before she finished teaching me."

"Your mother?" Meg interrupted. "But the bloodline comes from the O'Flahertys, your father's family."

"Aye, it does. But me mother was special… like she was one of them. She nurtured me as both her child and her student."

"Nanny…" Meg was unsure of herself and struggled to say the words, "I've met her—your mother. She saved my life and my friend's life, too. She is a selkie."

Nanny's face did not change. She simply nodded acknowledgement as if Meg had told her that the sky was blue or that they lived in Connecticut.

"Nanny, what is her name?"

"Shayla. Why?"

"Because I am going to see her again, and I'd like to call her by her name."

Nanny's face brightened with a big smile for the first time that day. As Shay was returning from the kitchen with the tea and cookies, Nanny looked at Meg, and said, "I know."

Made in the USA
San Bernardino, CA
04 December 2013